POWER PLAY

by

M.H. Vesseur

POWER PLAY

A RADIO DETECTIVE

A novel by
M.H. VESSEUR

Vibes Publishing

Published by Vibes
www.mhvesseur.com
www.facebook.com/MHVesseur

Second edition
ISBN 978-94-91908-39-2 (paperback, 2nd edition)
ISBN 978-94-91908-07-1(epub with DRM)

Power Play

One

The sun had done its job for the day. Obviously it had no plans to hang around a little longer, the way people do after work, for drinks or for chitchat or for sucking up to the boss. No, this old yellow star was steering straight down towards the horizon line of the ocean.

There was still about half an hour of light left, and in the long shadows on the surface of a container ship a tall man stood still for a moment. He pressed his back against the steel wall behind him and looked across the bay landwards. From the harbor area came the afternoon noises of boys on motorbikes running errands, reggae music from ghettoblasters, police car sirens, bar piano music, drunken tourists and the whole haberdashery. But it was distant, half a kilometer away, and the man kept on listening for a while to focus on sounds coming from the ship's interior.

This dark hulk was not the largest container ship in the world, but it was certainly a close call. It lay silent off the coast in the growing darkness, without drawing much attention, even if it was way too big to dock here. Other large ships anchored in this region regularly to take supplies onboard, like food and water, or to send their crew to shore for a few days off.

It was an old ship, rusty and scarred, but robust and nowhere near its final voyage — a bit like the man walking around the ship's deck. He was also large, and scarred in the face like old boxers can be, with a crooked nose and thick lips and an overall alignment that was slightly off balance. But he stood firm on his long legs. His short black hair seemed glued to his skull, in that typical manner of practical men: it's hair, and that's hassle enough.

Or maybe he'd just had a rough day so far and the hair had simply got into this state as a result of sweat and grease. Who knows.

When he was convinced there was nothing to be heard, he proceeded towards a cubicle, which stood alone on the forward deck of the ship. It was the size of an old-fashioned telephone booth, rounded off at the top, with a door on one side. The door gave way to a stairway leading down.

The man opened the door as slowly as he could, and then descended the stairs.

Sweat started to drip from his forehead.

Below deck, several languages were spoken simultaneously. As he came down the stairs, the tall man heard Spanish, Russian and English, and a bit of Afrikaans. The voices were approaching him.

He hid in an alcove in the dimly lit space under the stairs and waited till the whole group had passed him. He saw five men, strong, athletic and lean, with square faces and grim looks. They might have been telling each other jokes, but they certainly weren't laughing in response. They were all armed; some had a gun in a holster, others were carrying automatic weapons, one had a knife stuck behind his belt the size of a fish — the kind of fish you would point out when you are exaggerating your catch of the day.

He heard them climb the stairs he had just used to come down. A cold hand gripped his heart when he realized that he could easily have run into these men moments ago.

Then he was alone in the ship's interior. He walked along a corridor with no doors and then finally it ended. He felt the doorknob, pressed it down, and faced the interior.

"I told you," he whispered.

In front of him stood a hydraulic installation, black and dripping with oily sweat. It was as silent as everything else here, but it was a powerful piece of equipment, quite capable of making an ear-shattering noise when fully operational.

Then the man felt a hand grab his left shoulder.

Then, another hand appeared on his right shoulder.

Grabbing a tall man by the shoulders puts you at a disadvantage if you're not so tall yourself. Perhaps the two men in the ship's bulk were over confident, but it's safe to say they had underestimated the stowaway's physique. Not only did he tower above them, he was immensely strong and possessed an excellent condition.

He stuck both elbows backwards, hitting his opponents in their throats. Then both his fists moved backwards as well, landing in their lower parts with such force that they staggered backwards, not knowing whether to reach for their throats or that other sensitive part. Because when it comes down to the facts of life, it remains to be seen what part of the body is the most receptive to external influence.

Although they were disoriented and incapable of shouting, the men were not yet fully incapacitated. One of them stepped back, raised his automatic rifle and fired a shot into the ceiling.

The bang echoed through the metal interior of the ship, accompanied by the magnified thud of the bullet upon impact.

The tall man stood still.

People came running down the stairs.

Guns were pointed at the tall man.

"Bad idea," he said, smiling. He raised his hand and held up a lighter.

"No," yelled one of the armed men.

"If I light this," said the tall man, "we all go to heaven together. So you better put down all your guns and put your hands in the air. It seems I have nothing to loose, unlike you people, who have everything to lose."

All the men froze and started to put down weapons on the ground.

"Now you all pass me and walk over there."

When the last of the men had passed, the tall man started to walk backwards, picking up a gun from the floor on the way. He kept on walking backwards, stretching an arm behind him, until he felt the stairway.

Then he turned, just in time to see a huge fist hurl into his face.

Two

"No sake please. No."

This was the fourth time Hitomi Sakamoto, producer of the business talk radio show The Boardroom, had had to correct the waiter. For some reason the young man had concluded that she, being Japanese, would drink sake and that there was no need to ask first.

Truth be told, he held the same opinion about sushi and several other Japanese dishes — or dishes that were meant to resemble Nippon cuisine.

Under normal circumstances Hitomi would have made a serious issue out of all this, but not on this particular day. She did insist, however, that the young waiter switch the sake for an ordinary cup of tea. But she also smiled at his behavior.

Was taking a few days off finally getting to her head?

It had taken Hitomi a couple of days to get the gist of things. After being in this place for a while, she was actually beginning to relax and enjoy the sun and the leisure time, although she was still keeping an eye open for a topic for the radio show of her boss, bizz jockey Carl Pappas.

It had been a joint effort of Pappas and the WCBN Radio

general manager Phil Solo to convince Hitomi to take a four-day vacation, which had been a total waste of time until Solo finally played his last card and gave her two options: take a vacation or take a hike.

That was the kind of language Hitomi Sakamoto understood, and she had decided to leave Carl Pappas with the illusion that he had really convinced her.

And then again, by now, she was sort of happy that Solo had forced her. Her cell phone was offline and placed securely in the little hotel room vault and after checking with the reception seventeen times on the first day she had given up and was, wow, starting to relax.

The only vacations she had taken all these years of working for Carl Pappas had been trips to her birthplace, to see her extended family, but like the bizz jockey always said: that was also an obligation. A vacation is supposed to be free, even if that feels weird.

Behind her, the hotel rose on the hill of the sunny village by the ocean, all white plaster with pink shutters and a roof of green tiles. Around her was the terrace, quiet in the early morning — Hitomi Sakamoto was an early riser at all times — and in front of her, on the other side of a dusty road, was a vineyard of olive trees and a small field with goats trotting around. Further to the left was the village, built all the way down to the ocean. To the right were mountains, albeit not very tall.

In the street in front of the terrace, young men were standing by a low wall, their motorcycles parked orderly by the side of the road. It was unclear to Hitomi why they were here, but she guessed that maybe they worked in one of the vineyards and gathered early. She liked their energy, their laughter in the early morning sun, their eagerness to engage in just another day of local business. Nothing corporate, nothing big. Just the simple life. She also liked the fact that they had not been spoiled yet by the good life; these young men didn't need to go to the gym to keep in shape. They were athletic without striving for it.

She smiled while sipping her morning tea.

A man walked out of the hotel. An older man, tall and tanned, but skinny with a boney structure in his face, and the whitest hair Hitomi had ever seen. It stood up, almost without bending in the wind, like the man himself: proud and erect, dressed in a suit as white as his hair. He walked like a man who was unafraid, with a clear picture of where he was going.

He yelled something at the boys and they came running. There was some short conversation, some running in and out of the hotel, and then the whole party moved across the road. The boys were now carrying equipment, the purpose of which eluded Hitomi. It could be some giant kite, she thought.

She looked at the towering man in his white suit, leading the boys across the street in the direction of a large hill. The young men had lost their bravado; they now acted humbly in the presence of this man.

===

Hundreds of miles away a small boy was playing on a beach. His parents were only twenty meters away from him, sitting comfortably in their beach chairs. His father was reading an old paperback novel about sharks while smoking a cigar and trying to prevent the ashes from falling on his whale-like belly, and his mother was thumbing through a glossy magazine full of women half her age and half her weight. The boy sat in the sand in his screaming yellow swimming pants. His blond hairs rushed from underneath his orange summer hat down to his shoulders. He had the beach tools all kids have, plastic stuff like a bucket and a shovel; tiny tools, but huge in the eyes of any kid.

Slowly he moved into the water a bit, trying to dig the wet sand and pile it up in order to build something of a castle. For a while this worked quite fine, although he had to move fast to prevent the water from washing more sand away than he could dig up. But then he heard a roaring sound and as he looked up towards the sea he saw a wave towering above him that he hadn't seen coming. Of course he was sitting down and he was still small, so the wave looked impressive — and then it jumped on him and threw him backwards and dragged him across the sand, which really hurt.

He gasped for air and swallowed tons of water, but the wave was gone as fast as it had arrived — and then he found he was stuck. Something heavy pushed him down on the beach.

A man. A huge man was lying on top of him, and that was real scary and he started screaming and within seconds his parents were on the spot and the body was taken off him.

Only then did the parents realize that although their kid was alright, they had just lifted a dead man off of him.

"That's just great, Al," the woman hollered to her husband.

Three

When Hitomi Sakamoto reached the top of the first hill, after a stroll through the sandy, bushy terrain, a spectacular sight hit her eyes. Twenty huge wind turbines stood in a lower area, facing the ocean. They were standing in a relatively low terrain between the hills where the hotel stood, and the village, and the mountains some kilometers away.

The spot was meticulous: the oceanic wind was allowed to cross the island and generate some serious power. More than enough for the small towns scattered across the small stretch of land.

The tall man with white hair had moved his whole group to another hill that was laying head on in the wind blowing from the sea. Hitomi could see that the equipment had been unfolded too. A hang glider indeed. It must have been made in China, for it was obviously painted to resemble a dragon, a red monster with fiery eyes and some bright yellow flames around the edges. The man strapped himself to the hang glider and started running towards an edge. He was also carrying a backpack in front of him, attached to his chest and belly.

And then he jumped and sailed on the wind towards the wind turbines. Behind him, the young men cheered at the unexpected agility of this old geezer.

The tall man with white hair sailed smoothly between the turbines, staying way below the turning blades. Then he turned, and turned again.

And again.

And again, and Hitomi squeezed her eyes to see what he was doing, but it was unclear.

Then she understood: he was spraying paint from aerosols that he carried in the backpack hanging on his chest. Each time he passed one particular turbine, he put some paint on it, made a wide turn, and came back. The area was surrounded by a fence, which could be the reason he had chosen this unusual type of transport. But it seemed more likely to Hitomi that the man was giving a special performance. Instead of climbing a wind turbine and painting it, he had chosen to fly like a hero, to steer his dragon glider through the skies and impress some imaginary audience.

He was obviously an experienced hang glider, because he kept the right altitude and created a painting on this one wind turbine quite fast. Sometimes he had to make a wider turn, sail against the oceanic wind and climb before coming back into the turbine park — but he made no mistakes and worked meticulously.

Right in the middle of the wind turbine, halfway up from the ground, a deadhead appeared. It faced the ocean. Around its pale features, a black cloud appeared and grew larger and larger each time the man flew by.

When the entire middle part, about a third of the turbines

length, was covered in black, the man returned to the hill on the other side of the fence and landed, in his small crowd of cheering boys. From her distance, Hitomi couldn't see too many details, but they seemed to be heralding the flying artist.

She saw the man take off his gear, fold it back, and give it to the young men to carry. They rushed across the hill and disappeared.

Four

In the decades after the Second World War many derelict parts of the city had found a new life. Old buildings and trees and bushes had been removed and then offices, government towers, factories and apartment buildings had risen from the ashes of many years of neglect.

But time is never satisfied. Once this renewal had been completed, some of these new parts were abandoned once again as the years went by. So is the life of the metropolis: it blooms and then it withers away again.

Somewhere in these withered parts, on the outskirts of the city stood the remains of a circus. It had once been the property of the proud Griminaldi family. When it finally grinded to a halt, having been exploited by the family for more than two-hundred years, family head Orlando Griminaldi had taken his own life by entering the bear's cage in the absence of the animal trainer.

After a short police investigation the rest of the family and all the circus staff had been sent away, the animals had been transferred to the nearest zoo, and the tent, mobile homes, cars and the animal cages had been sealed, lock stock and barrel; then the gate had been sealed as well and that had been that.

But since no one showed up to buy the bankrupt enterprise, the circus had slowly been forgotten. It stood there on the edge of a forest, facing the city, but it was already hiding behind larges bushes and trees, fading from view.

In the main tent, a man stood still, trying to assess the interior in the vague daylight that came through the tent's roof and its many holes.

He looked like the son of a public official and a banker; a gray suit, a gray overcoat, a gray hat. But he stood straight, his chin up, looking into the darkness with his fierce, and also gray, eyes as if he were looking for an enemy. And his hair was pitch black, and his shoes were red.

Then a voice sounded, quietly, from the spectators' benches behind him. Way up there, on the stand, sat a man.

The man in the gray suit looked down at his red shoes first, sighed at the sight of spots from the dirt on the circus floor, and then walked up the stand. It wasn't until he reached the highest level that he could shake the man's hand and sit down next to him on the wooden bench.

Deep below them was the circus arena, an empty circle in a faded yellow of sand and canvas.

"Is this really a safe place to meet?" said the man in the gray suit. "Aren't all the city's hooligans walking around here?"

"You worry too much, Mr. Bercovitch," said the man.

He clearly had a Mediterranean accent; but it could be both from the north, the east or the south of that sea. He was a small, heavy-built man, almost without a neck, with a square black carpet of hair, a jaw that could function as an anvil, hands that were built for never letting go — but his suit was much more expensive than that of Bercovitch. And of course it wasn't gray.

"I have a couple of men walking around this place. But what the hell; it's mainly forgotten. City hooligans want to be in the center of things; they hate wandering out this far out. They fear they might get lost, you see? It's a shame nonetheless. The old Griminaldi Circus going to waste like this. A crying shame. That's what Europe has come to: they're letting their heritage go to the dogs."

Bercovitch shrugged. "I'm not sure if the circus is part of the European heritage. They've lost touch with the times, I think. People don't want to pay and see animals being treated cruelly."

"You are a sentimental fool, Mr. Bercovitch," said the man. "People have always loved to see it and they still do. But some parts of the world are taking political correctness to a whole new level. Pick up a whip and point at an elephant and at once you are a mass murderer. Makes me wonder if you are the right man for the job."

"I was wondering what kept you," said Bercovitch sarcastically. "Usually you fire your first insult right away. Listen, I started this operation twenty years ago, we're doing just fine. You know how far I've gotten things for you people. So save your nonsense for your bodyguards. Listen, I flew all the way because you have information about that man who is snooping around. So, tell me."

"He's been eliminated."

Bercovitch sighed again. "Is that wise?"

"Why wouldn't it be?"

"Well, as it turned out this man belongs to the circle of friends of a man they call The Don Quixote. A man with a wide range of fire; I just don't think it's wise to touch these people. It may attract attention instead of avoiding it."

"Who is... Don Quixote you say?"

"His real name is Lalo Schilverstein."

"Oh, well, we all know Lalo Schilverstein. Last thing I heard was... he had fallen ill."

"He recovered," said Bercovitch. He sighed once more and looked generally unhappy.

For some reason, unhappy people appear even more unhappy when they're in a circus tent.

A man appeared in the circus and started to walk up the stand. He was the bodyguard type.

"It's not good to upset people who are hard core environmentalists."

The bodyguard arrived at the nearest level. "We only have ten more minutes left, sir." Then he walked down again.

"That man, that Don Quixote as you call him. He's a lunatic. He is not worth your breath," said the man without neck. "You have done well, Bercovitch. I have also requested to meet you here to express the gratitude of all oil companies and governments involved. So far you have done the job extremely well."

"Do I hear a large 'but' coming there?"

"Not necessarily. Although there are those who... think it is time to replace you with someone new. Time to wipe out your traces and add a new level of invisibility to the whole operation."

"I will have to explain that to my government," said Bercovitch.

"There is no need for that. When the time comes, I will simply instruct them. I just want you to know that it is not a punishment, but a reward. You will be able to start living a normal life again. In the limelight."

"I may have forgotten just how that works. How to operate a normal business in the limelight, I mean. By the way, how is the work going with the new chairman of the United Nation's office for oil extraction? Has he been... brought over into our camp yet?"

"We are exerting the lowest amount of pressure as we speak. We do have some nice information about his past though, something that could be used to coerce him into obedience if the normal approach doesn't work. You see, we go to great lengths to convince people to work with us in harmony. Harmony is the word. Now, please stay here for ten minutes till I'm gone, Bercovitch. If all goes well, we will not meet again in this capacity, but on some party in Dubai, or a place like that. Like old friends."

They shook hands.

Then Bercovitch looked on as the man descended the stairs of the stand and walked across the circus arena, into the half darkness.

He sat there a lot longer than the required ten minutes, thinking about what had just passed. For some reason it felt like a big change was coming. Real soon.

A nice dark spot on his past, he thought. In the end they are all criminals, blackmailing people to do whatever they want.

He himself knew all about that. He could still feel the "information" hanging above him like a guillotine's blade. "Information" never went away, it stuck to you like a dog that bit you in the leg and wouldn't let go.

Finally he shrugged and got up.

No point in dwelling on things that can't be changed, he thought.

But he felt a chill going through the old circus tent, as if the ghost of the old Orlando Grimaldini was still haunting the place.

Five

Later that morning Hitomi was having her early lunch on the terrace, staring towards the ocean beyond the vineyard. A white blur appeared in the corner of her eyes.

"Will you excuse me, miss?"

She looked and stared right into the face beneath the forest of white hair. Even his eyebrows were white, and moving upwards in the same stubborn way as his other hairs.

"Please allow me to join you for lunch, miss?" His voice was a pleasant discovery for Hitomi, in a world where too many men — as far as she was concerned — talked either too loud, too high or too offhandedly. This man talked in a low voice, slow and clear, and melodious.

"Sakamoto. Hitomi Sakamoto. Please do, mister...?"

"Schilverstein. Lalo D. Schilverstein," said the man, while taking a seat on the other side of the table. "But please do call me Lalo."

"That would depend," said Hitomi.

"On what, Miss Sakamoto?"

"On two things."

To Hitomi, the man with the white hair did look like some

English Lord. She watched him wave at the waiter, and then turn to her again.

"Let's hear it."

"First it would depend on whether you will call me Hitomi, and second on what the D stands for," said Hitomi, giving him a modest smile.

"Hitomi, it would be my pleasure. And the D would be Don," said Schilverstein. "As in Don Quixote, I might add."

The waiter appeared and Schilverstein exchanged a few pleasantries, along with a menu order.

"Now, where were we?"

"You painted yourself just now as a kind of Don Quixote," said Hitomi. "One that attacks wind turbines instead of the old fashioned windmills?"

"A sharp observation, Hitomi, and precisely what I had expected of you. You are not from around these parts, I presume?"

"Surely you are not evading the topic at hand, Lalo?"

"I wouldn't dream of it, Hitomi."

"Would that be Sir Lalo by any chance?"

"No such luck. Although Her Majesty the Queen has suggested knighthood to me on several occasions. However, I feel such an honor would interfere with my current objectives as a, to get back to the topic at hand as you say, as a Don Quixote. Because yes, I do attack wind turbines. But in a creative way, as you have obviously witnessed your very self this morning."

"Aren't you worried that the authorities might come after you?" said Hitomi.

"No," said Schilverstein. "Usually they don't notice

anything for days. These turbine parks are abandoned most of the time. They have cameras but they never look at the images and if they did they wouldn't recognize me anyway because I wear a surgical mask to prevent myself from having to gasp in the strong winds. Someone drops by every fortnight in those wind turbine parks I suppose, but that's about it."

Hitomi laughed. "You make it sound like a routine job. Are you at this all the time?"

The man who called himself "Don" nodded tenderly. "Does that surprise you? There are many turbine parks along the coast and on several islands. I'm on a mission to send a message to a larger audience."

The waiter appeared with a bowl of salad from the local menu, and some juices to go with it.

While they waited for the waiter to finish and leave, Hitomi and the white-haired man looked each other in the eye. Schilverstein nodded again.

Then the waiter was gone and Hitomi said: "What message would that be?"

"Why, the unjust propaganda of wind energy as the solution to the world's energy problems of course."

"It isn't a solution then?"

"Well, there you are. People have come to believe that wind energy is nothing but good. To say anything that casts even the slightest doubt on this belief is like pointing a finger at a very sensitive religious group."

"Well, enlighten me then, Don Quixote. Burden me with your doubts. I'm all ears."

The Don ate some salad, took a sip from his pineapple juice and then said: "I know you are, my dear. You immediately struck me as a woman of the world. Well, it's not the wind that's the problem here. It's the technology of these turbines. There is a whole list of objections that is usually ignored or overruled. One: they are immensely expensive. Two: they are building too many of them at the taxpayers' expense, which means the chances of losing your investment in the long run increases dramatically. If you can't make a profit, the public will be paying for expensive maintenance for decades. Three: they are impossible to live with, because they make an amazing amount of noise, they hum in the night, they hiss. Also they pollute the horizon. I'm not sure if that's a big problem in a world where every major city has skyscrapers ten times the size of these turbines. But, nevertheless, you don't want a turbine park close to you. Also, birds are being killed by the millions by the turbine blades."

"Oh come on, Sir Don Quixote," said Hitomi, laughing. "Most of that may be a problem, but it still beats the pollution caused by the use of oil and brown coal and nuclear energy, wouldn't you say?"

"You disappoint me, Miss Hitomi. I expected better from you. You see, huge amounts of material are needed to build one wind turbine. It's all metal and plastics and copper and so forth. There's no such thing as clean energy from the wind. Surely it's an improvement from the old energy, the stuff we get from the soil, but it's just not such a good idea when most of these downsides can be avoided through the exploitation of solar energy. Why settle for an old-fashioned idea?"

"Old fashioned?"

"Yes. Don't forget that windmills have been around for hundreds of years. We can get the same results now almost for free."

"For free?" yelled Hitomi.

The Don moved across the table and put a finger on Hitomi's lips with such speed, that she spurred her eyes wide open and looked into the white of his eyes — again, surprisingly white. He looked around him. "We have to be careful, Miss Hitomi," he said, keeping his finger on her lips.

For a moment nothing happened. Hitomi moved her eyes left and right, saw nothing, and finally looked at the hand in front of her face.

Only then did Schilverstein remove the hand.

"We have to be careful for what, Lalo?"

The waiter appeared.

The Don lifted a hand with the palm up, looking straight at Hitomi.

Need I say more, thought Hitomi. He's giving the message: *need I say more?*

While the man with white hair dealt with the waiter, she contemplated how there would be no greater pleasure than to come back to the WCBN Radio Studio and present the editorial board with a story too crazy to believe. Her boss, the bizz jockey, would be absolutely delighted. Another killer topic for his business radio talkshow The Boardroom.

The waiter left and the Don said: "We are facing serious enemies of green energy, Miss Hitomi. Serious enemies."

She loved the "we" in that line. It had that adventurous sound.

After breakfast, Lalo Schilverstein took Hitomi to the harbor for a walk along the quay, where the old fishing boats lay undisturbed, bobbing up and down gently in the mild waves that the ocean brought here, and then they went to a taverna in an alley, a place that could not be found and seemed a little hostile towards strangers. But for the Don, rules seemed to bend themselves, and the people bowed with them, and so they could sit at a small table in a corner and have a drink and listen to the local music. Yet for most of the time, Hitomi was drowning in Lalo's stories, which seemed to flow endlessly, from his mouth, within her.

Six

A faceless celebrity among millions of listeners worldwide spoke again. It was the voice of a man in his forties, a deep, well-trained voice, a tad smoky, meticulous in its pronunciation, and also the official voice of WCBN Radio.

Like every weekday night at precisely 11 PM he hollered through the airwaves and onto the internet, followed by a slight echo that was added by the sound engineer. Bizz jockey Carl Pappas liked his introduction to be a bit operatic, for it created the right atmosphere, plus it allowed him to make a modest start himself. It was the classic "*here comes your host!*" approach. It also had a touch of a "*be amazed!*" announcement. It was one step short of becoming a "*small step for a man, but a giant leap for mankind!*" kind of thing.

"It's eleven o'clock. The city is dark, but the fire burns. It burns in the offices. It burns on Wall Street. It burns in the City. It burns on the Bund. It burns in Dubai. It burns in the factories and power plants. And it burns within us. Because we are the business and we all need redemption. This is the hour of delusion and today's truth. This is The Boardroom. Here is your prophet, the buddy and the bodyguard of every

CEO, the Don Juan of every business babe. Here is the world's one and only bizz jockey. Here is your BJ: Carl Pappas!"

And they were off. Many hours of preparation by the editorial staff finally paid off and took its final shape during this new hour of The Boardroom. All those preparations had been precise; a lot of what was going on had been carefully scripted — but the whole show felt like something that was entirely improvised nonetheless. This was the unique talent of Carl Pappas, the Bizz Jockey.

"Hi there, you business boys and girls around the globe. I'm all with you. I heard it's been a tough day. My WCBN Radio boss told me so. Anyone in a management position knows that the scandal that unfolded today once again blemishes the reputation of managers all over the world. It's too bad that a few rotten apples are spoiling it for the rest of you good people... That is, if you've been good. Which remains to be seen! Because I will be the judge of that, at least if you have the guts to show up on The Boardroom. No doubt a couple of you clowns and jokers will be calling me in a few moments to take a public beating on live radio..."

From the other side of one of the studio windows, his regular sound engineer Don Wozniak smiled. The smile included the donut he had been eating, and balancing on his fingertips while pressing his console during the opening moments. He shoved a piece of the food back into his mouth before it could fall out, smacked his lips and then lifted that same thumb to give the bizz jockey the *way to go* sign.

Next to him stood Hitomi Sakamoto, the show's producer. From the corner of her eye she observed what she was hearing, the sound of a man eating a donut and licking his fingers. She liked neither what she was hearing nor seeing.

For a woman like Hitomi, dealing with a man like Don was always a challenge. The whole point was of course that Don didn't care — except for that one detail that had been bugging him for years, which was that Hitomi Sakamoto was allegedly in possession of a natural six pack.

Hitomi, on the other hand, did care. She was a short, slim Japanese woman in her forties, a force of nature that kept in shape in the gym, lived like a saint and was unimpressed with virtually everyone she met. She wore her black hair either loose or in all kinds of ponytails. Almost all men who met her were attracted to her immediately and then fell into two categories: those who were wrapped around her finger by her charm, and those who were wrapped around her finger by her sharp tongue.

Sound engineer Don Wozniak was an exception because he just didn't care. He was the kind of guy who could say "I just don't care," and you'd be staring at his protruding lips, greasy from eating a donut or cold french fries from an old takeaway lunch.

He didn't buy her charm and he ignored her sharp tongue. He was much younger, in his early thirties, and while being a total beast about creating the perfect technical ambiance for radio broadcasting, he was careless in almost everything else. His hair was waxed into an upright position every morning, but it was done too sloppy to look like anything stylish; just a series of thick needles pointing in several direction, like a game of mikado with black sticks. He had a puffy face and a large belly to accompany it and a pair of thick glasses to emphasize his look. Around his console were the remains of potato chips bags, cola tins, plastic coffee cups and then there were clothes and hats and all kinds of paperwork.

In spite of that, Hitomi Sakamoto, who hated all this, always stood next to Don Wozniak's chair during the entire broadcast. She felt that was necessary because Don was the man who pressed the buttons. She wanted to be on top of him all the time, in a manner of speaking.

Luckily, Hitomi was one of those rare people who didn't think that work should necessarily be fun all the time.

"Should the government ever choose to pay this building a surprise visit to inspect it, we better pray they start on the ground floor and work their way up," said Hitomi, sounding as sarcastically as she possibly could.

"Mmm," moaned Don while he sucked his thumb once more, "and why is that?"

"Because then we'll have time to rush in here and clean the hell out of it before they enter and declare it a clear and present danger to the national health."

"Oh, you mean like Chernobyl?"

"No. I mean like the Ebola virus," said Hitomi.

Neither of them laughed or even chuckled. They focused on the man in the studio before them.

"Today we are talking energy. Before you say, hey, you do that all the time, I must tell you this: we have some new perspectives and new ideas coming up. But before we go into that, I have to tell you about this CEO I know who's in the energy business. He chairs a solar panel company. Hard work, big profits, taking over the world, you know, going for a good thing. So, one day he comes home and his wife is in bed with the pool cleaner, some younger dude. So this CEO is shocked, you know, he's like, what *are* you doing? What are you *doing*? And his wife says, and she's not even stopping, she says you're putting all this energy into solar panels, every bit of energy you got goes into these solar panels. So now I got him to put some energy into ME for a change!"

Don Wozniak burst into laughter, putting tiny fractions of donut on the studio window in front of him, much to Hitomi's dismay. She herself didn't laugh; she had been opposed to the joke from the moment she read it.

Jokes were a delicate issue on the show. Some were made up by Carl Pappas himself, others were made up by the show's main writer, Job Messner. But Hitomi fought no fights with these men, because she felt she probably didn't have the sense of humor that it takes to appreciate this level of banter.

Meanwhile, the first caller was put through to Carl Pappas.

"Hi, I'm Ron and I command an oil platform."

"Hi Ron. Well, that puts you in the heart of tonight's topic. You got a contribution to this show? Something you'd like to drill home?"

"Well, yeah, I want to say that it's a miracle there are no more oil disasters. We've barely got enough funding to operate, but the safety standards have been lowered."

"And why's that?"

"Because too much money is going to other kinds of energy."

The bizz jockey laughed. "Are you saying that using *less* oil is potentially bad for the environment?"

"Exactly my point. Oil industry bashing comes at a price, my man."

"Don't you call me my man. I am not your man. How dare

you blackmail the world on my show. You know as well as I do that we *have* to look for other sources. This is not a mere question. It has to be done. After centuries of growing rich, it is now payday. So stop whining and take your responsibility. Crank up your oil platform safety, Ron!"

He moved his hand in the air across his throat — so Don disconnected the phone call from the live broadcast before the caller could respond.

Opposite the bizz jockey sat a man with white hair.

Seven

"I have a dead man on my hands."

Those were the words whispered into Hitomi's ear, earlier that day, when she had gone down to the WCBN Radio building lobby to greet the Don. As they hugged and kissed, his lips touched her ears, and whispered: "I have a dead man on my hands."

He also looked concerned. But he didn't say anything else until they were in the elevator.

"A friend of mine, who is dedicated to the same cause, has washed up dead on the shore," said the Don. "Clearly he was on the trail of something big. They killed him."

He raised his voice a little when they went into the elevator.

"He was investigating the companies behind every wind turbine park in the world, looking for clues."

"What kind of clues?"

"He thought that by looking at the ownership worldwide, he could detect a pattern. For instance, if a significant number of turbine parks are owned by oil companies, that would mean something."

Hitomi looked puzzled.

"Oh, it doesn't matter. I'm not saying I followed his drift exactly. Perhaps he was just being paranoid, but he was a green energy buff nonetheless and he said he was on the trail of a major fraud. Now he's dead and there are bullets in him."

Then Hitomi had emphasized that this was not something the bizz jockey should hear about right before the broadcast started.

So Hitomi went up to the seventeenth floor where she walked straight into the bizz jockey's office with the tall, white-haired man in her wake and announced the arrival of an important guest of tonight's show.

"Carl Pappas, Lalo Schilverstein, also known as... the Don," she said.

"Delighted to meet the world's one and only bizz jockey, Mr. Pappas," said Schilverstein, marching past Hitomi with his arms stretched. He grabbed Carl by both arms and squeezed hard. "I can't believe I'm finally standing in front of the one man in this world who must undoubtedly agree with me."

"Is that so?" asked Carl.

"Why, yes, of course! You know of my current quest?" asked Schilverstein.

"No, not really," said Carl. "I usually confront my guests with my own mindset, not theirs."

Hitomi interfered. "The two of you meeting before the show is an exception. Actually it's not really for the purpose of the show, it's just that I feel you guys must meet. Period."

"Hitomi tells me you are against wind energy," said Carl. "You're against the pollution of the landscape by the sight of turbine parks?"

"No. That's irrelevant. My point is that compared to the incredible ease of obtaining energy from the sun, wind energy is costly and polluting. It is serving neither the economy nor the planet to our best ability. Wind energy will always be expensive because it is based on the use of turbines. Whether on land or on the sea floor, constructing them is costly. Solar panels need none of that complicated technology and the price of solar panels has been going down for decades, and will continue to do so. What's there to choose?"

The Don pointed out the window towards some giant office towers in the distance. "Look," he said, suddenly lowering his voice and talking like he was about to reveal a conspiracy, "there are your oil giants. Those are their ivory towers. I can assure you they'd follow my every move if I let them. They are scared as hell by the green power development. They hate it. So, they are scheming against it."

The bizz jockey sighed. "You're not paranoid I trust?"

"No," said Schilverstein. "Look, that building is occupied by the COPCAN, the Crude Oil Producing Companies and Nations. Ever heard of it?"

Both Carl and Hitomi shook their heads.

"Remember that name. They are as inconspicuous as they are dangerous. It's a whole bundle of governments and corporations devoted to keeping oil in the center of things."

Hitomi walked out of the room to take care of the imminent live broadcast, and leave the men to their discussion.

The Don's dead man would have to wait.

"The lack of progress in the development of true green power is a crying shame," hollered the bizz jockey, right after he had introduced Schilverstein to his audience. "Too many governments are waiting for other countries to act first, saying they don't have the money and their economies can't bear the burden. The energy giants are sitting in their lazy chairs. Consumers are putting more and more money into wind turbine parks, but the economic value of these is volatile. I cry every morning at the thought of this lack of progress. My girlfriend is about to walk out on me because of it. The hardest people to get on The Boardroom are the oil energy CEOs. It's been two years since we had one. But tonight we are talking to a famous green power activist, also know as the Don, ladies and gentlemen in present you Lalo Don Schilverstein. Welcome, Lalo."

"I'm delighted to be here."

"What's your take, Lalo? You just explained that the investments in turbine parks are a step in the wrong direction. But don't you agree that anything that takes us away from brown coal and oil is a good choice for the time being?"

From behind the window, Hitomi looked on, uneasy. The Don's dead man was still waiting.

Eight

It goes without saying that the presence of Lalo Schilverstein on Carl's radio talk show The Boardroom was nothing less than an honor. In business circles, the man was still a legend, albeit a bit faded.

Before slipping on the wet surface of a hotel shower cabin and sustaining a serious concussion, many years earlier Lalo Schilverstein had been a model businessman. He had been an example to follow. He ran four companies on three continents in the capacity of general manager or owner or CEO or CFO and he did that with skill, without mercy.

In fact, when asked about the secret of his success, he often joked: "I prefer SM."

And then, when faced with a speechless interviewer, he would add: "By applying the right amount of skillfulness and mercilessness, I have arrived at the top. Being merely without mercy is for people who thrive on destroying things, like warlords. But I am a builder. And as a builder, I thrive on my skills and the skills of my people. The mercilessness comes second, like the icing on a cake."

He was, of course, referring to the process of hostile

takeovers, the ruthless acquisition of businesses. A process for which one simply had to be without mercy — it was all about eating or being eaten.

A smooth man with an entourage of managers and bodyguards, hurling across the globe in a corporate jet, raiding and acquiring and selling, with no apparent end destination in sight. No marriage. No children. Living in different apartments in the cities of the world.

Until that day when he slipped in the towering Manifesto Hotel in his suite on the 130th floor, on a November morning, when the fog was covering the city below his window. Down there, in the gray cloud, men were crying, no doubt, for they had lost their business to the predatory team of Lalo Schilverstein.

Perhaps it had been Lalo's excitement over the takeover that had been completed the day before. Perhaps it was a slight hangover. Or perhaps the shower cabin had not been scrubbed clean properly, and a small amount of grease on the bottom had caused the international businessman to slip and fall and bump the back of his head against the water tap.

When he woke up, he didn't remember his fall. He didn't even notice the small bump on the back of his head until many days later, but for the rest of his life he would fail to make the connection between his slip in the shower and his renewed outlook on life.

He sat at his breakfast in the hotel dining room, wondering why he had this incessant headache all of a sudden, and what these young men and women — dressed in black and white and nothing else, wearing designer glasses, rectangular without exception — were talking about.

What the *hell* were they talking about? he wondered.

He could not figure out why talking about all this money and all these profits and all this collateral damage could be important.

It was not like a *new* Lalo Schilverstein emerged. No, it wasn't like that. For he remembered everything that he had done.

It was just that numbers had lost all meaning to him. Until that moment, he had been talking numbers every day of the week, including the weekends. Anything any member of his staff ever did, needed to be justified through numbers. Someone did something? Then that someone had better explain the gross profit of that something. What was the gain? There had hardly been a single conversation in his life without numbers.

But that morning, it sounded utterly ridiculous and boring to him.

"Did you see the match yesterday?" said one of his team members, before he sipped some coffee from a hotel-design cup.

"I sure did," said another. "That guy can add a digit to his net worth."

It not only puzzled him, it filled him with disgust.

Then he noticed something peculiar. There was a little card standing on the breakfast table that read: *The Manifesto Hotel is proud to announce that the combined food leftover of all our dinners has been reduced by 50 percent in the last twelve months. We thank our guests for participating in our Save Food Program.*

Lalo had read the message over and over again, and

suddenly his headache had gone away as if it had melted, then had felt invigorated. He had felt thrilled.

He left the table, looking for more of these uplifting, beautiful messages. And when he couldn't find enough of them, he decided to create some himself by fighting for a clean, healthy world.

And to wake people up to do the same.

Nine

Funny how you suddenly start noticing things, when they have eluded you all your life. It's like having burned your back in the sunshine; all of a sudden everyone you meet seems to want to pat you on your shoulders. That's how the mind plays tricks on you.

This is also how true paranoia emerges.

Carl Pappas, to name one, had never paid any attention to the sand- colored office building that stood close to WCBN Radio. It was a nameless skyscraper, albeit an elegant piece of architecture.

But this morning, after he had parked his car in the WCBN garage and walked across the pavement towards the Gulag to meet someone, he decided to turn some extra corners. Upon passing, he looked at the entrance of the sand-colored building and noticed there was, indeed, a sign that read COPCAN, and underneath it Crude Oil Producing Companies and Nations.

In mid stride, the bizz jockey stopped. He thought about the accusations that Lalo Schilverstein had made last night on his show, all vagueness without any facts to back up his story.

But this unique man, this "Don", had made an indelible impression on Carl nevertheless. Now he looked at the tall building with fascination, thinking about the many times he had passed it without seeing it.

Now he saw it.

And now he saw a story, a conspiracy, a danger.

Right there and then, out of the entrance of the COPCAN building, a familiar face emerged.

Although familiar was probably too much — here was a man Carl Pappas had met in the past on several, unrelated occasions. Not really an acquaintance or a friend. Just somebody from the business world.

"Bercovitch? Ben Bercovitch?" Carl said loud.

The man looked at him and then stopped. "If that isn't the Bizz Jockey," he said. He walked over to Pappas and shook his hand. "Hi Carl."

"Hi Ben. Did you... just come out of this building?"

"Yes. Does that make me... a suspect?" Bercovitch asked.

"Of course it does," said Carl, without laughing, just to test the water. "This is the COPCAN building."

Ben Bercovitch was very quick to throw a smile in for good measure.

"I can vouch for COPCAN, Carl. I know there's some activists who hate our guts, but it's all with good intentions plus it's good for all the economies involved. That should appeal to you, being a major promoter of doing business and making money and creating jobs."

Carl pointed to a fountain in front of the entrance. They walked towards it and sat on the edge.

"You've gained some weight, Ben. And I mean that most

literally. Has working for COPCAN introduced you to the good life?"

"Not as good as yours, I suppose."

"How's that?"

"Well, working for the oil business is increasingly becoming a hazardous job. There are aggressive activists these days. If I go to a birthday party, I'm always attacked."

"Verbally, I take it?"

"So far."

===

"I've done some checking," said Lalo to Hitomi.

They were sitting in the radio lobby on the seventeenth floor, occupying comfortable leather chairs in a dimly lit hallway. People were rushing through the hallway, talking on cell phones and not paying any attention.

"It's not so far from where you and I met. Some five hundred kilometers. An island quite like ours."

Hitomi smiled at the suggestive sound of "ours" in the Lalo's message. "That's close to the mainland," she said.

"It is. But the significant part is that it is also, for a large part, a nature reserve. It's one of our government's largest nature reserves, actually. And now comes the interesting part: they've built a huge turbine park right in that reserve."

"That's not a problem, is it?" asked Hitomi. She felt the chilling shade of boredom — was Lalo going to keep going on about schemes in the energy world? She hoped not. She was going to have to kick him out of the building if he was.

"Not necessarily," said Lalo. "But my friend did say that he was on to a grand scheme hidden amongst energy giants and that it had something to do with wind turbines. Now here" — he took a map out of his jacket and unfolded it — "is one of the largest nature reserves in this part of the world. It's completely closed to the public. It has one of the largest wind turbine parks in the world. And my friend, who was investigating the turbine business, washed up dead on a shore near this place."

"I don't know, Lalo," said Hitomi, doing her utmost not to sound uninterested. "They could be loose ends. Unconnected. You're not asking me to... propose this to the editors of The Boardroom, are you?"

"Far be it from my mind to ask you something like that," Lalo said, his face flushing with dignity. "What you people do on the radio, well, that's none of my business. But I do want you to fly with me to this island and help me investigate. You have the skills. You have the connections."

"So do you."

"Nevertheless."

"I will decide tomorrow morning. Now you must excuse me."

Hitomi stood up and immediately she received a strong hug from the tall man with white hair. "You are so deliciously resolute," Lalo said loud. "It excites my heart!"

Then he turned and walked away, leaving Hitomi speechless for a moment.

Ten

That very same evening, Ben Bercovitch was already appearing on The Boardroom.

"Being a government official and all," said the bizz jockey, "you have shown remarkable grace by appearing on my show and talking freely about this institute called COPCAN. That's the Crude Oil Producing Companies and Nations. What a name! Now we have practically been neighbors for a while and yet I've never heard of you people. Why has COPCAN been operating in the shadows?"

Bercovitch smiled and then added a sound into the microphone to make sure the audience understood that. "We're not consciously operating in the shadows, Carl. It's just that COPCAN is an entirely diplomatic organization. It functions as a messenger boy between companies and nations, but yields no real power."

"I find that hard to believe. If only for the building you're in, it's too large and too expensive," Pappas said, and his tone was one of a man who was challenging an opponent.

"Think about express delivery companies," said Bercovitch. "They have the hugest headquarters. It's nothing special. We do research, we check all data from oil extracting operations, the refining, the distribution and so forth. We share this information, we talk to governments who want more money from oil companies, we negotiate about the acquisition of areas were new oil fields are found..."

"I get the point," said the bizz jockey, a bit rude. "I believe you."

"We also do not have a press department, no public relations people, no image, not even a logo."

Both men laughed.

On the other side of the window, Don said to Hitomi: "What's he up to? Isn't this kind of boring?"

"Just wait," said Hitomi.

"I have another question," said Carl. "A couple of years ago one of the world's largest new oil fields was discovered right under a national park on the island of Islasol."

There was the tiniest moment of silence.

"You must remember that. You know, as you were responsible within COPCAN for negotiating such a new location."

"Your research is excellent, I must say. But I can assure you, Carl, that it was not 'a couple of years ago'. It was more like twenty years."

"Why is that park closed to the general public, Mr. Bercovitch?"

Behind the window, Hitomi smiled mildly at the sudden chilling of the bizz jockey's voice.

"Well, I'm not an expert on nature reserves, Carl. I'm the wrong man," said Bercovitch.

"O come on. We found out that COPCAN has tried to

negotiate the installment of an oil drilling installation there for a whole year. Who stopped you?"

"The government owns that park. Some reserves are closed to the public because they offer shelter to vulnerable animals and plant life. You know: a little peace and quiet from tourists?"

"But isn't it a bit strange that one of the world's largest wind turbine parks was built on *top* of that oil field, in the middle of that nature reserve?"

Another moment of silence.

"On the contrary, Carl. Because this turbine park has been put on top of the oil field, there is no point in further debating the extraction of oil. It's the perfect solution: we get energy from that land, but we leave the oil down there."

"The government, our government, owns that reserve and the turbines?"

"I don't remember. Like I said, it's twenty years ago. As I recall we had to abandon the oil field and that meant closing the file on Islasol."

Carl slammed both hands on the table.

Hitomi grabbed her elbow.

"Why would COPCAN try to talk about extracting oil from a nature reserve to begin with? Isn't that a pointless exercise? Isn't the answer supposed to be 'no' right from the start?"

"I wasn't involved in this particular... endeavor. I don't know."

Much to Hitomi's surprise, the bizz jockey decided not to pursue the matter further.

"Well, thank you Ben Bercovitch, for appearing on The Boardroom and telling us about COPCAN."

He made his gesture and Don Wozniak made a tune magically appear out of nowhere.

A soft curse came from Hitomi's lips.

"What?" said the sound engineer. "Did he say something wrong?"

"What do you mean, 'something wrong'? The man hardly said anything! I mean, is there anything you know now, that you didn't know before Bercovitch came on the air?"

Eleven

The small aircraft had been in the air less than three hours since taking off from the airport close to WCBN Radio and it was already making its final descent. The island of Islasol, its destination, was close to the southern coast and too small for large jets — there was no major tourism industry and it possessed nothing of political or economic significance.

So Lalo Schilverstein had rented a small plane to go there and check out the circumstances of his old friend's death.

"Remember we are nature lovers and we want to be in the proximity of the nature reserve, Miss Hitomi. And you are *not* working for the radio. Can you do that?"

"Are you asking if I can fake?" said Hitomi.

She looked Lalo in his eyes and he looked back.

"Far be it from me to say that you fake. You are a lady. Think of it as *theater*."

Hitomi turned her head quickly to hide a smile and looked out the window at the airstrip on the edge of a long island. "Are you not, by now, a famous face? To a great many people you are the face of environmental activists. A businessman who made a fortune, who is now painting skulls on buildings and turbines and oil platforms, like a modern-day batman under his giant hang glider. Aren't you worried you'll be recognized on Islasol?"

They were shifted up and down in their seats as the small plane jumped downwards towards the concrete.

"You flatter me, Miss Hitomi," said Lalo. "I have done a few stunts, yes. But if I am famous it is only in the business community. My work as a skull painter has not yet reached the media — and hardly anyone knows I am the man with the kite. So I think we are safe from discovery. We will have to be careful though, my old friend got killed in these parts, remember."

"Presumably."

"I'm very comfortable presuming."

The hotel was small and located on a hill, offering a splendid view of the ocean and a part of the island. The landmass was shaped like a crescent moon, and in the distance, along the curved coast, they could see the thin silhouettes of the wind turbines.

"A quiet place," said Hitomi.

They were standing on the roof terrace.

"There's nothing much happening here. There are a few villages, that's about it. People don't like to travel here because it's essentially a dry rock in the sea."

"So where does all the electricity go that comes from the turbines?"

"Part of it is transported by cable to the mainland. It's on the other side of the island, and not so far away."

In the waters near the village, some sailing yachts and

small fishing trawlers floated.

"And what's that over there?" asked Hitomi, pointing towards the horizon.

The Don made a swift movement and a pair of binoculars magically appeared. "Now, let's see."

After a glance, he gave the binoculars to Hitomi and said: "Interesting."

Hitomi looked and saw the gray, unclear silhouette of a container ship.

"You may have noticed it's not moving," she said after a while. Then she dropped the binoculars. "Perhaps it's out there waiting for something?"

"Who knows," said Lalo. He rubbed his thick mass of white hair, which withstood all rubbing and winds and continued to stand up. "My dead friend did say something about large ships as well. I don't remember the details, I'm sorry to say. I didn't think much of it at the time because, well, he was indeed a bit of a paranoid. He saw conspiracies everywhere."

"Unlike you?"

Lalo smiled and put a hand on her shoulder "Surely you are mocking me. I know I suspect governments and business to be tinkering with the truth, to be involved in schemes that can't stand the cold light of day. But I always abandon these suspicions quickly, if I can't substantiate them. I prefer to engage in real action. You know, action leads to reaction. But my dead friend, he has been pursuing mirages for years."

"Was he ever right?"

"Sometimes, yes. Therefore I am taking this very seriously and prefer to keep the authorities out of it. We're on our own now, Miss Hitomi. If I am right, he discovered something in this area and got killed for it. So keep your eyes open. Now here is my first plan of action."

===

In the middle of the night Hitomi woke up for no apparent reason at all. She walked to the balcony of her room and stood there for a while, taking in the still warm night air. After a while she noticed the container ship. It was still in the same place, way in the distance. It was flooded in light.

"You're seeing it too?" a voice said close to her.

On the balcony next to her, Lalo stood. He leaned over the railing and gave her his binoculars.

"It's too far away too see any details, but I can assure you these lights are not for walking the deck. These are spotlights meant to create a daylight ambiance. They're at work."

"What work?"

"You name it."

Twelve

It wasn't quiet very often in the Gulag, the small diner standing on the banks of the river that flowed through the heart of the city. But this was definitely one of those days.

That may have been a perfectly good reason for Mach One to meet the bizz jockey here, at the small table by the window overlooking the river. He disliked crowded places — too many dangers lurking. The more people around, the bigger the chances of running into someone he didn't want to run into.

As an extra precaution, Mach One had taken on a disguise. He was wearing a wig instead of his old hat, he had grown or attached a full beard additional to his mustache, and he had left his brown raincoat at home and wore an accountant's suit instead. His large bulk put serious pressure on the buttons of his shirt.

To Carl's amusement, he also spoke with a cockney accent.

Not that anyone was there to hear it; there were no people and Mach One was speaking very softly. Only Kate, the owner, was around, popping up at their table every now and then to fill their coffee cups.

"My dear Katharina Yekaterina," Carl said, "how beautiful

you look today. It is a shame there are hardly any customers to admire your grace. The good side is I get to take it in all by myself."

"Please leave some for me," said Mach One. "We may be in the Gulag, but I am free to do some admiring myself, no doubt."

Kate laughed. "Thank you, gentlemen. I will cherish all the attention that's coming to me — if I can find the time between motivating my cook and serving the customers." At that, she winked, and walked off.

"A fine woman," said Mach. "She reminds me of a time when I was in Russia. I was in Yekaterinburg, you know, where the tsar and his family were held during the Russian revolution in 1917."

"How does she remind you of that?"

"There is something tragic about her power," said Mach. "She appears to be in complete control of everything, but I sense a sadness that is kept under the surface. I'm sure you can get her to dance and sing and drink vodka at the same time, but you will never get her to spill her guts. It's either a real sadness that is hidden deep, or it is an imaginary pain. Like a melancholy: it has no other origins than the Siberian ice fields. A wind blows and makes you wonder what it is all about."

Carl Pappas sighed. "My my, for a moment there I thought we were never going to have a romantic, poetic moment. But there you are! Shall I ask Kate to sit down and join us while you bring up memories of things past?"

It was virtually impossible to annoy Mach One. He just smiled at Carl's remarks. "You have never been to Russia, my friend. You just have never been."

"I don't exactly feel the urge. You're painting a pretty good picture anyway, so why should I bother? I can see it now, the wind howling through the birch tree woods. That should make a man melancholic, let alone a woman!"

"Cough up the story, bizz jockey. Before this talk gets to us," said Mach, grabbing his coffee cup and bringing it to his mouth.

"There's a gigantic nature reserve on the island of Islasol that is closed to the public," said Carl. "Within its perimeters is one of the world's largest wind turbine parks. I need you to look into the chain of ownerships."

"Good," said Mach One, smiling, wringing his hands.

Looking into the chain of ownerships was an example of their own, private jargon. For the benefit of The Boardroom they had discovered many interesting stories behind large corporations and organizations simply by looking into who really owned them — all the way down the chain. Some people went to great lengths to hide the true owners, through shell holdings on obscure islands in the Caribbean, off the coast of China or India, or in Switzerland or the Middle East. But someone who was familiar with these invisible trails, who was also tenacious, would eventually reveal the true ownership — someone like Mach One of course.

"Isn't that simply the government?" he asked.

"I think so, yes. But we need to know nonetheless. There's an oil field right underneath that turbine park. It was discovered two decades ago but after years of legal battles they decided to put this park on top of it. But it's all very secretive. Why is the public not welcome in this park?"

"A nesting place for vulnerable species," said Mach. "There are a lot of these resorts, worldwide."

"Find out which vulnerable species," said Carl. "If it's a park for animals and plants that are about to go extinct, you're surely not going to put a turbine park on top of it, are you? That doesn't really make sense."

"It does if it's a windy spot," said Mach. "Why is everybody always so stressed out about taking some energy from nature?"

Kate arrived with new coffee.

"Good question," said Carl. "Why is that?"

Carl and Kate both looked at Mach One expectantly.

"Hey, don't look at me," he said. "There must be a sentimental reason for it. And I never get sentimental."

"My kind of man," said Kate, pouring the coffee.

"And such a liar," hollered Carl, much to the other's amusement. "A moment ago you were crying at the mere thought of Russia."

"Was he now?" said Kate.

"I was not!"

"I don't know," said Kate. "Men who are really not sentimental, usually never even use that word."

===

The ocean pushed its waves gently towards Islasol's rocky coastline. The small sailing barge was lifted up, kept on moving upwards for a while and then slid down a wave, all very slowly in the afternoon sun. The boat hardly moved. There was no wind to speak of, so it took Lalo and Hitomi two hours to get close to the large container vessel. They had dressed themselves up as tourists, wearing Hawaiian T-shirts and white hats and large sunglasses. Hitomi wore a short jacket that puzzled Lalo.

"Is that a judo outfit or something, Miss Hitomi?" he asked, when they were floating a mere two hundred meters from the container ship.

By now they could see that the ship was a monster; like a black wall rising from the ocean floor.

"It must be loaded to the brim," said Hitomi. "It wasn't a couple of hours ago. Don't you think that's strange?"

The Don looked at the bulk. "You are a remarkably perceptive young woman," he said. "The darned thing is much deeper in the water now."

Then he pointed to another large ship that was approaching. "It's also getting company."

An hour later the two ships were lying side-by-side.

By that time, Hitomi and Lao had sailed in different directions, staying well clear of the two giants. They observed from a distance, through binoculars. There were other sailing boats and fishermen's vessels, and to make sure no one would pay a lot of attention they drank wine and played some music from a ghetto blaster. It was also a way to kill time.

"How come you never married?" Hitomi asked at one point, when the wine was becoming comfortable and the obvious talents of the Don for sailing the boat safely across the waves had become sparkling clear to her. Lalo Schilverstein was in perfect condition. His advancing age had clearly been halted by a spartan lifestyle, she concluded.

"I am not the marrying type," said Lalo. "I have done my businesses, I have been in politics and now I am into the environment. Women want to have children. I would rather not be a father than be an absent father to my children."

"Where's it written that you have to have children with a woman?"

"It's written in their eyes," said Lalo.

"Surely not every woman's eyes?"

"No, I guess not," said Lalo. "Sometimes I just have to look a little bit closer to make sure I am not mistaken." He moved closer to Hitomi, on the bench, and looked her straight in the eye.

The afternoon heat was fading, and so was the light, and the air smelled like frangipani, even if the coast was at least two kilometers away.

For a moment, Lalo was convinced the frangipani smell was coming from Hitomi, and for a moment he thought that the further opening of her eyes was a good sign, as was her enormously deep breath — the deepest sigh he had ever heard.

Then he heard the cracking of glass and a scream woke him up from his daydream.

Thirteen

The office building lay in green fields, a concrete block of only two stories high with as much elegance as concrete could have. The sun played on the white plastered surface and mirrored itself in the large windows on both floors. Hundreds of cars were parked on the lawns surrounding the building, their multitude of colors making the place look like the stalls of a fruit market.

But below ground level, in the building's cellars, twilight ruled across miles and miles of archives, carton boxes and folders. There were fluorescent lamps above every corridor of racks, but they were old and gave only a pale light.

Two men were walking through the corridor. One was talking without interruption — he was dressed in a brown duster, his thin gray hair was exploding on top of his head and his glasses gave him a surreal, alienating look, his eyes bulging in a way quite fitting for an archivist. The other man was not talking at all — he wore a long, black raincoat, his hairs were greased and combed back and he showed no expression on his face.

Suddenly, the archivist stopped. "Why anyone would want

to look at the original papers when they're all available in our digital archive is beyond me," he said. "You one of those old paper fetishists? You want to inhale the dusty smell they give off? What's your angle?"

"The digital realm cannot be trusted," said the visitor. "So I always do a reality check first. Can you point the dossier out for me?"

"Here are all the files of the oil field under Islasol," said the archivist. "They've been buried in this basement for twenty years by now. You can see how the boxes are all dusty. It's this whole shelf. Well, what exactly do you want to look at? I'll leave you to it. There's a table over there, I'll get a chair."

The old archivist turned and walked away, but he was struck on the back of his head with such force, that he fell to the floor immediately.

The visitor took a small package from his coat, put it on the shelf, and then took a small clock from his pocket and attached it to the small package. He turned the clock and while it started ticking, walked off through the long corridors.

In a corner of the basement, he reached a door. With a thin pin he took from his coat, he opened the lock and disappeared through the door into a pitch-black void.

Within seconds a firestorm erupted from one of the shelves behind him and an inferno was born, way too powerful for the sprinkler installation to deal with.

===

The next morning, on the hotel terrace, Hitomi gave Lalo Schilverstein a piece of her mind.

"From now on I will assist you with your planning," she said. "I thought you knew what you were doing, but you were not thinking clearly when we were out there last night."

"Oh come on, Miss Hitomi," Lalo laughed. "Neither were you."

"That ship would have run us over if I had let you carry on with that romantic looking into my eyes stuff."

"You were getting romantic yourself, don't forget that. You saw the ship by accident, that's all."

"I was simply paying attention."

"You saw the ship's reflection in my eyes, that's where you saw it. Admit it, Hitomi."

Indeed, they had had only seconds to start the engine, turn the boat, and catch wind in time to sail away and escape the steel wall of the first container vessel that had been steaming in their direction. Hitomi had crushed a glass in her hands when she realized what was happening.

"These ships must be incredibly powerful, to be able to make speed so quickly."

The Don smiled at Hitomi's obvious attempt to change the topic.

"So, tell me your plans," Hitomi insisted.

"Very simple," said Lalo. "I'm getting my hang glider and my spray paint ready, first of all. Then I must check if the equipment is safe. In the mean time you can read the maps and check the surroundings of the wind turbine park for hills, for a good place to take off, for fences and so forth. Then there's the weather forecast — well, all of that."

"And what about the search for your dead friend? Where is he anyway? In the local morgue?"

The Don looked towards the horizon. "No, he's already been shipped out. I don't know how, but I'm not really that interested. I know enough details. He was shot. There were oil stains on him. And considering the currents of the ocean around that time, it is obvious he was coming from the general direction of these container tankers. He has been shot in that area, no doubt about it."

He took a last bite from a croissant on his breakfast plate, wiped his mouth and wanted to rise, but Hitomi gestured him to stay seated.

"There you have it, you attack like a maniac, trying to do everything at once. Are you here to find your dead friend or to attack wind turbines? It is very unpractical to do both at once, you know. We need to focus here."

"I am focusing, Miss Hitomi. By painting my famous skulls on these turbines, I will draw out whoever is behind all this. If his death has anything to do with the turbines, I will scare them and then they will show themselves."

"And if nothing happens? I still don't see what you are expecting to accomplish over there."

"Neither do I. And if nothing happens, we will go back out to the ocean and dive and see what's going on underwater with these ships. Can you live with that, my dear Hitomi? And if you can, may I please be excused?"

Hitomi waved a hand to acknowledge. "Sure."

They both got up.

As they walked away, the waiter overheard Hitomi saying: "I just wish you'd make up your mind. You can't say Miss and dear at the same time. It's very uneducated."

"It's just a bit of versatility, my dear Hitomi," the tall

white-haired man could be heard saying.

===

Ben Bercovitch was not feeling too good. He had his reasons.

Some of these reasons were relevant, others were not, but that's always the point with feelings: you can get upset as much about the trivial as about the important.

His situation at home was irrelevant, although it upset him enough to cause his stomach to protest. His wife was getting enough of him. And if that was hard to deal with, he was currently unable to do anything about it. His work at COPCAN was going to absorb him even more in the coming months, while he felt he should really spend more time at home and fix things. Mrs. Bercovitch had grown chilly, if not cold on him, and he had reasons to believe a competitor was at work while he was away. In a way it made sense to him, but she was too much a trophy wife to give up without a fight.

Anyway, all that would have to be postponed, because now he had made a bad appearance on The Boardroom. Now that the bizz jockey had asked him about that stupid island of Islasol. He had done some stammering and avoiding, and his bosses were extremely pissed off by it all. Now he had been ordered to smooth over whatever needed smoothening.

He really wanted to call a private investigator to spy on his wife, but he decided that there were more important matters that needed his attention; the kind of stuff that can kill your career — or even yourself.

Then a cell phone rang from his drawer. He pulled out the drawer and took the call.

"Bercovitch."

"..."

"All the original charts of the oil fields are gone? Well, it's the biggest overkill I've seen in years. Burn the whole archive down, are you nuts? Don't you think that draws way too much attention? And what about the digital archive?"

"..."

"OK, well, that sounds good. Nothing on the internet?"

"..."

"That's the good thing about pre-internet stuff, I suppose. OK, stay close to your phone. I have a feeling this is not over yet."

He put the phone back in the drawer.

Now it was time to do a bit of waiting.

He thought about hiring a detective again, but quickly discarded the whole idea. No need to pay a man to come up with proof of his wife's adultery. Next thing you know a private eye shows you some nasty pictures of the Mrs. in all the wrong places.

And then again, it was a small worry compared to his problems at COPCAN.

He picked up the cell phone again and dialed a number.

"..."

"Ben here. Be warned that there may be people nosing around on Islasol."

"..."

"I know. But this time it's very dangerous. These are big media people. I'll try to find out more, but you better make some calls and get people to pay attention. I mean: real attention. Make sure they're armed, but also make sure they're not too eager on the trigger."

Fourteen

Mach One was also known to the bizz jockey as Ross York, but that was presumably just a pseudonym. Nothing Mach had ever told Carl about himself had ever made any sense, and nothing had ever been confirmed by official sources. At some point Carl had inquired through one of his secret service contacts, as casually as he possibly could, but they had made it perfectly clear there was not a living soul called Ross York that matched the description of this slightly overweight man with a scar on his upper lip that was partially covered by a mustache.

Not that any of this mattered. Mach One was the fastest private investigator you could possibly imagine. Whatever request Carl Pappas made, it was always executed swiftly and precisely by this secretive man, who worked only directly for the bizz jockey himself. None of the members of the editorial staff of The Boardroom knew anything about it. Producer Hitomi Sakamoto was vaguely aware of a secret contact that was being used to get deep information. Boss Phil Solo had an even foggier notion. That was it.

The investigation into the backgrounds of the national

park on Islasol and the wind turbine park had generated quick results, as Carl had anticipated.

"It is too complicated to explain in detail," Mach One said on the telephone. "All you need to know right now is that there's a group of people operating on a local level. They're a curious lot, to say the least."

"Hit me," said Carl.

"The man in charge of local operations is an ex-convict. I happen to know his background. His name is Arthur Albuquerque, but don't let his fancy name fool you. He has been working for some serious criminal organizations in the distant past. Supposedly that's all behind him."

"What's so special about him?"

"He's one of the top organizers in the world," said Mach. "Complex logistical operations that need to be kept secret from the public eye is his specialty. He is not even officially working for the government over there. He is paid through some offshore company, and he keeps a low profile. But the mere fact that he works on Islasol is telling enough."

"I'm not sure where that leaves us, Mach," said the bizz jockey.

"The other things I found out are equally disturbing. There is no record of the oil fields that are supposedly there. The state archives where all this was stored, were severely damaged yesterday in a fire. The digital archives have been compromised."

"Can't some oil company cough up some old files?"

"Come on Carl," laughed Mach One. "You'd have to put a gun to their heads to get any information. It's also two decades ago, it seems like the whole thing has been covered with dust. The other thing is, well, the ownership of the wind turbine park is complicated. On the surface it looks like a government operation, with ties to the local power company. They use the electricity that is generated. But the businesses that have built the park are shrouded with secrecy. They're all owned by foreign companies, which are owned by foreign holdings and so forth. It's a labyrinth."

"I'm not sure where that leaves us. What if I asked you to speculate?"

There was a sigh on the other end of the line.

"Come on Mach. What is Hitomi doing with this Lalo Schilverstein over there? They're looking into the death of a friend. Is that connected to all this? I'm not paying you to lead me into a labyrinth. The least you can do is take me by the hand when I go in."

===

And that was precisely what they were doing now: Mach One was taking the bizz jockey by the hand and led the way.

They were on board a small aircraft on a direct flight to Islasol, talking through their options.

"You don't have to pay me for this," said Mach One, uncorking a small bottle of sherry on the small table in front of him. He had just devoured a chicken salad, showing no signs of airsickness, even though the flight was rather bumpy.

Carl sat uncomfortable in the next seat. He hadn't touched any of his food.

"I am dying to find out what this is all about," said Mach. "This is by far the most complicated maze I have seen in my life. There is no doubt in my mind that something is going on at Islasol. At the same time I can't make anything of it. But I feel there are too many parties involved. It's just not normal."

"It's also not normal for you to come along on this trip," said Carl. "Any special reasons?" He looked at Mach One.

"Nothing that concerns you," said the investigator. "I'm in the information business and I have a feeling there's a lot to learn that I can use." He then moved his chair in the comfortable position, took a sip from his drink, laid back and put his hat over his eyes.

Message clear, the bizz jockey thought.

===

A thin man stood at the harbor of Islasol. He had his reasons for looking angry, and so that's exactly what he did. The ocean in front of him was quiet in the afternoon sun, and the quays were quiet. Behind him was a small warehouse that was once used for storing fish. A sign on the front read *Sea Service Ltd.*, but that was nothing but a facade.

He was listening through his cell phone to a contact of his business on the mainland and he did not like what he was hearing.

"On that plane is the bizz jockey, the host of The Boardroom, and we have reasons to fear that he is mingling."

"Anything in particular you want me to do about it, Mr. Bercovitch?" the thin man said with a voice that betrayed boredom rather than irritation.

He was as thin as a man could get without looking like a junkie or the victim of an eating disorder. His hands and face were boney; nothing more than a structure with an old, leathery skin attached to it. But he looked powerful nonetheless; he stood up straight and his dark eyes radiated with full force. His black hair was combed backwards and tied to a ponytail. His suit was that of a dockworker, kaki and worn. He would not draw any attention and that was how he liked it.

"That is more your line of business," said the voice on the other end. "I'm coming over. If these people are really on to something, we have to act fast. Don't wait for me; take some evasive action. I'll be there within twenty-four hours."

The connection was terminated.

Nitwit, thought Albuquerque. What kind of instruction was that?

He decided, there and then, to deal with the situation by applying swift force.

Then he walked back to the building, stepped inside and whispered his favorite line from an old Soviet dictator: "No man, no problem."

He allowed himself a short chuckle.

It always worked.

Fifteen

The sun was setting on Islasol when a small aquaplane descended in front of the harbor.

From the dark harbor front, where old buildings slept in the early evening, an object hurtled towards the plane with incredible speed. It was difficult to spot, because it was small — so none of the plane's occupants saw it coming.

They heard a short roaring burst, and then the left floater exploded. The whole machine shuddered, the windows shattered and the plane made a sharp left turn while it lost one of its wings. Then it hit the surface and whipped up a fountain of salt water, white and creamy in the fading sunlight.

===

Everybody was shouting or talking, trying to be heard above one another.

Until finally Hitomi Sakamoto shrieked something very loud — no one knew exactly what it was she said, but it had the desired effect. They all stopped shouting and talking.

"We have to leave the harbor and get to the hotel," said Hitomi. "If you guys were really hit by a rocket, it's probably not safe to stand around too long. Follow me."

The local police had shown considerable reluctance when it came to accepting their version of what had happened. There was no proof of a rocket attack on the aquaplane that Carl Pappas and Mach one had been flying in, and if there was any proof it was now on the bottom of the ocean in front of the harbor. Diving to the bottom to look into it was going to take days, they said, and who was going to pay for that? It was probably just a malfunction, they said. We will put that in our report for now, they said.

As they walked up the street towards the hotel where Hitomi and Lalo were staying, Mach One whispered to Carl Pappas: "I propose we do not pursue the matter for now. We came out all right and we need our time to prepare for more troubles. Best strategy would be to attack head on."

"Attack who?" said Carl.

He was about to find out.

The plane had dived into the water with its nose down. It was fortunate that the machine had been slowing down, so they hadn't hit the surface full speed. It had been a painful landing nevertheless. There had been glass all around, they had been slammed forward in their seat belts and then wave after wave of water had gulfed over them through the broken windows.

Within seconds they had found themselves in a sinking plane.

The pilot had hit his head against the yoke and Carl fought with the clip of his seat belt.

To his amazement, Mach One had reached over and undone it with a swift movement of one hand only.

By the time Carl had been out of the plane and swimming, Mach One was down behind him, rescuing the pilot.

A couple of hours later they reassembled in Hitomi's room. All but Mach One.

"Where's your travel companion, Carl?" asked Hitomi. "I thought you would introduce us."

"So did I," said Carl. "But he had a job to do."

"Anything we need to know?"

"Listen Hitomi," said Carl. He was tired of everything that had happened to him today and the clothes he was wearing were uncomfortable. The hotel owner had arranged dry clothes for him and the pants were too short, the shirt was too large and the shoes were too old. The colors, if there ever were, had faded long ago. "We are not preparing a broadcast, so you can relax. He was only a fellow passenger, you see."

"So was he under attack, or were you?"

Lalo raised a finger. "Obviously the arrival of the bizz jockey has made some people here very nervous."

"Listen guys," said Carl. "What if we're out on a limb? What if all this amounts to nothing? I feel pretty silly about this whole conspiracy theory. Governments and oil companies working together on some kind of energy scheme? If it's not ridiculous now, it will be real soon!"

He looked in the mirror above the fireplace in the old room, a Spanish hacienda kind of interior. "I'll tell you what's looking suspicious right now. Its my hair!"

It did appear as if he had been electrocuted: after his

involuntary swim he had neglected to take care of it. It pointed in several directions.

Lalo went to the cabinet to fix drinks. "I suggest we take that as an omen rather than a joke."

Sixteen

Mach One felt like a young boy again, as he sneaked through the darkness of Islasol.

The coastal town had been deliberately kept in the dark ages. The main road had proper streetlights, but there were plenty of alleys and small pathways that were hardly lit.

Mach One moved in the darkness through a maze of small houses and palm trees and rhododendrons and finally found a small boarding house. It was vaguely lit by the only lantern in hundreds of meters and had a sign on the front: *Paraiso*.

It had been a long time since his last days in field operations. He hadn't been planning to return to active duty again, because he knew like few other men just how dangerous this work was. Nevertheless, he wanted to stick his nose into this strange affair himself, because he believed it would bring him significant inside information. And now that he was out here, he felt an old excitement coming to life again inside him.

This is it, he thought. This is where my man hangs out. Now it's time to see if my information is accurate.

He moved into the alley next to the boarding house until

he found a service door. With a few quick movements of a magic key he opened the door and tiptoed inside.

He arrived in the kitchen of the house, which was only lit by a nightlight. He walked through it slowly and quietly, moved into the hall and up the stairs.

On the first floor he quickly found the room he was looking for. It was number seven. Here he repeated the trick with the key and slid into the room.

Once he was inside, he said: "Well, Arthur Albequerque, fancy meeting you here."

There was a rushing of blankets and cushions, a click and a bedside light was switched on.

Arthur Albuquerque looked into the barrel of Mach One's gun.

"You!" he croaked.

"Keep your hands on top of the blanket, where I can see them."

The gun was awfully close to Albuquerque's head. He had not been sleeping very long, and as he was a light sleeper as well he was alert enough to be shocked by the appearance of a long-forgotten acquaintance. "I thought you'd stepped down from active duty," he said.

"What do you care?" said Mach.

"Well, you sound unfriendly. If I knew you were still in the field, I might have retired myself. Got a little house on a beach in the Indian Ocean, gotten married and settled down."

"You haven't the balls for it, Arthur. All you can do is go in and out of jail, and it looks like you're preparing for your return to another penitentiary right now."

"Don't think so, mate." Albuquerque raised his arms.

"Look, I'm going to sit up straight, you see? Don't get nervous now." He knew he was talking nonsense, for he had never seen Mach One nervous in his life. When he sat up with a pillow prepped up against his back, he took a band from the bedside table and started to organize his hair and put it back into its ponytail design.

"Man, you look like a plank. You were always thin, but never this much. That from smoking too much or working too hard? Let me guess."

The thin man put up a fake smile. "You always were an asshole."

All of a sudden, Mach One was hovering over him, pushing his head against the wall behind him with a slam, and pressing the barrel of the gun ever so gentle against his right eye. "I have two questions for you. I need to know who ordered you to blow up Pappas' plane and what exactly you're paid to do here on Islasol. Either you answer these two questions for me within ten seconds or I'll have Interpol move in within the hour. You choose."

"That hurts," complained Albuquerque. "I need that eye."

"You can take the eye with you when Interpol comes to pick you up," growled Mach. He pushed the gun slightly. "Talk now. I've no more time for chitchat."

He kneeled on the bed, leaning on Albuquerque's knee with one hand. The weight was considerable.

Less than ten minutes later the thin man was tied like an Egyptian mummy, chained to the bedpost. Only his eyes and nose were not wrapped in sheets.

"Forgetting is the talent of the wise, my dear Arthur,"

whispered Mach as he turned towards the door. "It would do you a world of good."

Then he was gone.

Seventeen

In the semi-darkness, while the sun stirred below the horizon before another day, Lalo Schilverstein and Hitomi Sakamoto stood on the terrace. They were checking their backpacks and making last minute arrangements.

Behind them, in the doorway, stood Carl Pappas and Mach One.

"I need to leave this island right now," said Mach. "I have all the information I need."

"What about the information I need?" complained Carl. "Is the reason why you're not telling me because I am not paying you? I can pay you. Who assaulted us on the plane? What's going on here?"

"It's all very dangerous," said Mach. "There are several large organizations at work here and it is just possible one or more governments are in on it. I have dealt with the man who attacked us, so you will have a few hours to go out there and look into things. But that's it. No more. Go there, check it out and be out of here before the end of the day. People may be on the lookout."

"On the lookout for what?"

"The stuff this guy told me is too ridiculous to believe," said Mach.

"So where does that leave us, Mach? You run off because you don't believe it?"

"If the government is involved, it's going to be difficult to warn anyone. It's just... I don't know. It's simply ridiculous. To tell you the truth, I believe they're only stealing some electricity from these turbines. It's theft on a large scale, and maybe they're doing it all over the place, but it's not so big a deal. Not big enough to try to blow up the bizz jockey, right?"

"I still say the plane thing was an accident."

"Just stay with Schilverstein. He's savvy enough. I trust him."

Mach One shook his hand. "Take care, Carl." Then he disappeared into the dark hotel interior.

"Your mysterious friend is off again, Carl?" asked Hitomi. "Is that the average amount of help you get from him?"

"He's not the type for field work, I must admit," said Carl. "But I have no idea what drives him. Anyway, he said we have only a small window of opportunity before more people are alerted."

The Don stretched his arm towards the dark hills. "Let's go then. I want to be at those turbines when the sun goes up and not a minute later."

The darkness was not a great help. A small path led them away from the coast, into the hills, but it was a rocky route that put them at risk of falling, or worse.

They had decided to move without lights and without noise, so they walked slowly through the pale landscape, which was lit only by a half moon. But it worked out fine, although Carl Pappas and Hitomi were almost constantly whispering to each other.

"If your secret man says there's danger, why aren't we asking him for help? He seems to know more than we do," snapped Hitomi.

"He's not exactly going to say yes all of a sudden," whispered Carl. "Trust me."

"Then why don't we ask the government to move in? People who are armed at least?"

"Because the local government may be in on this," whispered the bizz jockey. "No need to alarm anyone until we can make a move. What are you worried about? We're just checking things out, that's all. Walk in, sneak around, get back. Once we're on live radio then we're in charge."

Hitomi halted for a moment and pushed a finger in the bizz jockey's chest. "Carl Evangelos Pappas, you are a dangerous man. I must be crazy to go along with this."

"Oh come on Hitomi," said Carl. "We're trailing behind Lalo. He's the man with the plan anyhow, and you are going with him rather than me, don't you think?"

The answer came quickly.

"Yes indeed," hissed the Don. "But that is no reason to make so much noise. You two are talking too loud and the last thing we need is echoes drawing attention. So please be quiet for just a little longer. Do settle your business disputes later."

Hitomi's face darkened. She shot Pappas an angry look. Then she turned and followed the leader again.

Behind her, Carl Pappas, the bizz jockey, chuckled as he tried to keep up with the two people in front of him. They seemed to be getting in a hurry.

At the same time he noticed that the hot and still night air was beginning to stir. A wind had begun to blow, every so subtle, but crisp with freshness.

It was fresh going on chilly.

It was a change, the bizz jockey thought. There was something in the air.

"Very convenient, this sudden wind," whispered Lalo to Hitomi, outside Pappas' earshot. "It will make my flight so much easier."

Eighteen

On the high ridge of one of the hills between the village of Islasol and the wind turbine park, they could see the ocean lying in the deep. It was hard for them to stand here, in the strong air current that tried to push them off the hill.

The moon played its tricks with what they saw, turning the ocean into an immense platform of unpolished chromium, stretching towards the horizon under the stars.

No more than a kilometer from the coast lay two immense container ships side by side, their noses towards Islasol. Trouper beams lit the decks in a bright white light, but other than that they saw nothing. It was too far away.

"They're keeping busy," said Pappas. Then he closed his mouth quickly, because a rush of wind had gulfed into his throat and made him gasp.

"Come on, people," said Schilverstein. "This is no place to hang around."

He had started to look like a real Don Quixote, his white hairs being kicked around by the strong wind, each one of them seemingly having found a life of its own. They all were grabbing around his head, touching, feeling, looking for an escape route.

It made the bizz jockey smile when he looked at it.

But not for long.

===

A few moments before dawn, Ben Bercovitch stepped from a small craft onto the rope ladder that was hanging down from the bows of the *Leviathan*. The large container ship was still in the dark waters off the coast of Islasol, undisturbed by the ocean. For days on end, the weather had been calm and the waters had been flat, but that was changing.

But Bercovitch didn't notice that and neither did anyone else. Not because the change wasn't noticeable, but because none of them cared.

As soon as Ben stepped on deck, he barked to the man who helped him by giving him a hand.

"Why can't I reach Arthur on his cell phone, oak? Is he here?"

The man stood still. "No he's not here, Sir." His upper torso was so solid and elaborate that he was called "the oak" behind his back — although there was no need for such secrecy, because the man was very proud of this nickname. Not that he needed a nickname like "oak" to emphasize his strength.

He was ogled by the new arrival.

The oak simply looked back.

"Anything you want to tell me?" said Bercovitch. "Any news about last night? Like can you give me an update on things?"

"No news from the island, Sir. There's been no word since late afternoon. We're basically carrying on business as planned. If that's all right, of course."

"No that's not all right," Bercovitch yelled. "He should have given word about any progress he made. Are you not... informed?"

"Informed about what, Sir?"

Around them, several men had gathered and were looking on. Bercovitch sighed deeply. He thought for a moment.

"Is that why you came, Mr. Bercovitch? You could've checked with me on the radio..."

"And have the whole world listening in? Haven't you got instructions to maintain radio silence at all times?"

Bercovitch seemed to have made up his mind and returned to the rope ladder. While he started to climb over the railing, yelling: "Come with me. I need you on the shore. On the double."

Then his foot slipped on the greasy edge and he fell. His crotch hit the railing and there he sat, holding on, like an uncomfortable traveler on the back of a donkey.

But he didn't shout and he kept his face straight. The oak moved forward and helped him across the railing, onto the rope ladder.

Bercovitch felt like someone had hit him with a hammer between his legs. He had the bizz jockey to thank for this humiliation.

Below, a small boat waited, its outboard motor roaring.

===

It was as if the earth had been sliced here. It was just an abyss two meters wide and fifty meters high, moving through the rocky landscape like a desert snake.

"It is a safe way," the Don had said.

But now they were not so sure anymore. Every now and then a few pebbles fell from the rocks high above. There were also many strange sounds.

"Were those, like, wolves or something?" whispered Carl.

"Carl Evangelos Pappas," snapped Hitomi, "stop acting like a wimp. Wolves live in northern countries. Not here. These are the subtropics."

The bizz jockey followed the two silhouettes on the bottom of the canyon, where the moon was basically not looking at all. "If I were a wimp I wouldn't be here," he murmured. "It is obvious Lalo Schilverstein has lost his mind long ago and that you are his equally oblivious groupie. I am the only one thinking straight and I tell you we better be careful down here. There may be predators. Listen!"

He stood still and did just that.

The others walked on.

The bizz jockey resumed his path and, looking up, noted to his relief that the sun was coming close to the moment where it would rise above the horizon.

He was now also beginning to doubt his own sanity too.

Was that a roaring sound ahead?

===

After a while, the canyon gave way to a more open space, with a river running through it. Silver fragments of the moon danced on the fast-moving stream.

"Great," said Carl. "A river from hell. How are we supposed

to get across that? Don't think for a minute I'm going swimming or something."

"Swimming is out of the question, my dear bizz jockey," whispered Lalo. "But as it happens, this river goes underground for a while and in one of these caves we can cross it and get out on the other side."

Now Carl reduced his voice to a whisper too. "My dear Don Quixote, surely there is no point in crossing a river in some underground cave, if we can cross it above ground?" He looked triumphantly, even though his expression of triumph could hardly be seen in the early dawn.

"The point is, we want to get to our destination *unseen*," said Lalo. "The underground passage takes us as close as it gets."

"I thought this turbine park was unattended, my dear Don," growled the bizz jockey.

"It is. The only fence they have is this river, and lots of difficult terrain around it. No guards. But I like to be on the safe side, my dear bizz jockey."

"Gentlemen," said Hitomi, her voice a couple of degrees warmer than usual — which in her case, meant quite a warming up, "please quit the friendly banter. I believe we need to move on. The sun will go up within half an hour."

Nineteen

The old warehouse on the quay was hiding inside the long shadows of the rising sun.

It had once been a busy harbor, but those days were a fading memory. There were just a few fishermen left, who set sail to catch fish for the local market only. Some sailed for the benefit of tourists, although there were only a handful of those. Somehow, Islasol had not made the transition into the entertainment age. The town's council was reluctant to spend money on advertising local attractions such as the mountains and the reef, which allowed great diving. They had also effectively kept all hotel chains off the island so far.

So on this morning, nothing much was happening on the cobblestones. There were two seagulls sailing overhead, screaming like a middle-aged couple with severe domestic problems. Below that, albeit less noisy, were the sounds of men shouting from the interior of the old warehouse.

"We need to find Albuquerque right now," yelled Bercovitch.

He stood opposite some bulky guys. They were all — except for the oak, of course — intimidated by his hollering, even if he didn't really have the voice for it. His vocal cords were not strong enough to deal with this kind of stress, so his voice went way too high and occasionally made a frog's leap into oblivion.

"We will split up," said the oak, trying to calm the boss down. He sensed that without his local representative, being Arthur Albuquerque, this Mr. Bercovitch was too agitated. "You and I will go to his hotel, the rest will check the other places he visits. Maybe he got drunk and he's lying on the floor of some bar."

Bercovitch looked at him, but he said nothing.

"Although I doubt he'd be that stupid though," nodded the oak.

===

The earth looked like a bed of nails for the gods; dozens of wind turbines stood in the rocky bottom as if someone had nailed them down. Each of the thin machines drew a long shadow on the rocky bottom of the landscape. Their rotor blades were thin compared to the vertical structures, but these were spinning round with a vengeance nonetheless. The night had begun quietly and without any wind, now it ended with a strong current coming from the ocean.

They were one step away from a gale.

The noise was immense. The small group of trespassers could proceed without any fear of being heard.

They walked down the slope and onto the flat terrain that formed a resting plateau for the turbines. There were dozens of them, so they split up and each checked a row.

Finally they walked back up on the hill where they had come from and shared what they had seen.

The noise from the wind and the turbine blades presented them with a small problem: how to communicate with one another? They tried to solve this by standing very close and putting two ears close to one mouth.

Hitomi and Carl brought their heads together as close as they could, so the Don could shout at both of them simultaneously.

They quickly decided that the turbines appeared to be normal and there was nothing special about them.

"I'll put on my gear now," shouted Lalo. "Then I'll proceed with my clownish act of putting some very appropriate deadheads on these machines. Propaganda for the masses. If anything is going on here, that will draw out whoever is behind it. And if it stays quiet, it will still be a successful operation because the deadheads can be seen from the ocean and will no doubt draw attention from the ships and descending planes."

Hitomi touched his arm. "Isn't the wind becoming too strong, Lalo?"

"Yeah," said Carl. "What's the danger here on a scale from, say one to ten?"

"I prefer a scale from one to a hundred if that's alright with you," said Lalo. "And the danger right now would be thirty on that scale. Just enough wind to help me move fast, but I'll still be commandeering my hang glider myself. But I must admit, if it gets any stronger, I may have to abort."

The man with the white hair took off his gear, put it all on the ground, donned a pair of goggles and then unfolded the hang glider with such agility that it left Carl and Hitomi speechless. Within moments, the giant wing was hovering over the Don as he walked back a couple of dozen meters to create the right amount of distance for his run-up towards the edge of the hilltop they were standing on.

"Don't you think this wind is getting too strong?" shouted Carl in Hitomi's ear. "Maybe we should stop him, for his own safety, and call the whole thing off."

His producer smiled one of her smiles, an attractive mix of rarity and mystery. "No one stops the Don," she whispered.

The bizz jockey couldn't hear her, but he read her lips.

I guess it's part of the man's glamorous attraction to the ladies, he thought. This mild insanity, this self-confidence, this willingness to challenge fate. This wild white hair dancing around and this dangerous business of flying a hang glider under these butcher's chopping blades.

But he smiled too — for a man like Lalo Schilverstein protected the world from becoming too predictable, too boring. And that was worth something.

The tall man had turned and was running towards them. He saluted them by touching his goggles with two fingers and then he took off. He was way up in the air before he had even reached them, or the edge — the wind simply lifted him up after he had run a couple of meters.

He took off like a rocket.

Neither Hitomi nor Carl Pappas, the bizz jockey, were smiling now.

Twenty

"Like I said on the phone at least three times," the boarding house owner said while his face dripped with utter contempt, "I have no idea if Mr. Albuquerque is in his room. It's none of my business, you see? And it is none of yours. It's called *privacy*, but that is probably a word you people have never heard of."

The oak bent over the counter and grabbed the owner by his tie. The furniture made a loud cracking noise, and also a ripping of clothes could be heard.

"Leave the man," Bercovitch snapped. "Up to his room, quickly. Listen, what's his room number?"

The boarding house owner looked angry but didn't speak.

So the oak shook him. He did that with such force, that a phone, a pile of magazines and a coffee mug fell off the desk. Also the owner's hairpiece and glasses ran for cover.

"Sevente-heen, seco-hond flo-hoor" the man moaned.

The oak then released him and he disappeared behind the counter with a lot of noise, while the contents of the cupboard above him — a whole series of telephone directories — started their descent.

By that time Bercovitch and the oak were already running up the stairs. The oak took the lead and by the time Bercovitch arrived on the second floor, all out of breath, the door of room seventeen was already hanging in its hinges like a retired circus acrobat.

The COPCAN official rushed into the small room, just in time to see Albuquerque being freed from the cloth that was tied over his mouth, his chains to the heater, and the ropes that tied his arms and legs.

Immediately Albuquerque started cursing, but the long hours with the cloth in his mouth had dried out his throat. His only utterance sounded somewhat like Yoda with a cold.

But these were men who could do without a sense of humor. So no one laughed. The oak lifted Albuquerque up the bed to allow him to recover.

"Sit still and don't get agitated. Allow your blood stream to reboot or you will pass out," he said with a tone that allowed no counter arguments.

"Who did this?" asked Bercovitch.

The oak turned, poured a glass of water from the bedroom sink and gave it to the victim.

"The man with many names," Albuquerque coughed. He poured the water down his throat, gulped it.

"What do you mean, many names? Speak up man, who was it?"

"I'm telling you he's the man with many names."

"Tell them!"

"Ross York. Henri Washington. And that's only two. I don't know his real name, I don't know what name he is using now. Hell, I ain't even seen him in twenty something years. I didn't think he'd be... doing field work anymore."

Bercovitch sat down next to his local foreman. "Listen, Arthur, listen carefully. I need to know, and I need to know now, is this man working for a government, for organized crime or for, well, for who?"

"For all I know he is for hire," said Albuquerque.

Bercovitch raised both arms very high in the air and then slapped them both down on his knees with as much force as he could muster. "A fine state of affairs. A bloody fine state of bloody affairs."

"Could be working for anyone then," the oak growled. "We need to get to him before..."

Behind him, Bercovitch was pacing the room. "By now it is perfectly obvious what's going on. You were trying to stop the bizz jockey from nosing around on Islasol. Perhaps... you have been a little bit overzealous and attracted the wrong sort of attention. You have been silenced so the bizz jockey could proceed. The question is: what does he know and where is he? Heaven knows how far they've got."

"If you're right, they can only be heading for the park," Albuquerque said with a dry, croaking voice. "I tried to stop him, make it look like an accident." His thin structure was shaking from exhaustion. "But can you shut up a talk radio host to start with? How many people will come looking if he disappears?"

"Now wait a minute," said Bercovitch. "He's just looking around, doesn't suspect a thing, hasn't got a clue. We just need to act fast and make sure nobody does anything stupid. Let the man look around. He's going to see zilch. Only if one of your men" — he pointed at Albuquerque — "loses his nerves, only then are we in danger of exposing the operation."

The oak and the thin man looked at him.

"Let's be practical about this. We've had people checking out the turbine park before. Entire legions of environmentalists and government officials and nature lovers. They all came and went and nothing ever happened. You get back to the warehouse and try to reach these idiots and tell them there's people poking around. They have to stay put for a while. Shut down operations if necessary. Don't make a sound. Don't move a muscle."

They started for the door.

"Better call the guys on the ships as well," said Bercovitch. "And go over to the Park to check things out before Pappas and that Don get there."

Before they left the room, they looked back and noticed Albuquerque. The thin man had fallen backwards on the bed.

"He's passed out," said the oak.

"I can see that. Well, what are you standing around here for? Pick him up. We can't bloody well leave the man on his bed!"

While the oak walked to the bed and started to shift Albuquerque on his shoulders, he mumbled: "He's so thin, nobody will notice him anyway."

Twenty-one

For Hitomi, the sight of Lalo Schilverstein rushing through the air hanging under his giant hang glider was nothing new. But even though she had witnessed it before, the scene still took her breath away.

The big wing moved swiftly on the strong currents, making large curves and sliding near to a particular wind turbine standing close to the ocean. Each time he passed the turbine shaft, the Don turned his kite so that the wing hovered almost vertically and he was able to spray some paint on the shining surface.

"Is he putting on another deadhead?" yelled Carl into Hitomi's ear. "I wish I could see it."

From where they were lying in the grass on top of a hill, they could not see the actual graffiti image the Don was painting.

"Yes," said Hitomi. "It's a standard image, always the same."

"When he's done, I want to walk over to the other side and see it up close. It's awesome."

"Yes, he's a regular Don Quixote," said Hitomi. Her voice

would have betrayed sheer admiration, but the noise from the wind and the turbine blades obliterated the words before they could reach the bizz jockey's ear this time.

As it turned out, the winds worked in the Don's favor, moving him around fast between the turbines, climbing and descending on the currents, turning back, and back again.

Suddenly, Hitomi kicked Carl's side with an elbow. It made him utter a loud cry of pain.

But before he could complain, he looked in the direction she was pointing and forget about the discomfort.

A series of land rovers was entering the area from the direction of the village of Islasol. They were driving very fast, drawing large clouds of dust that whirled into the wind above them like ticker tape.

Had the Don finally, by flying around like an ancient, winged warrior, drawn out the feared opposition?

"The cars are full of thugs," Hitomi concluded, putting the binoculars away.

By that time, Lalo seemed to have noticed their arrival too. He turned his hang glider away from the ocean, up with the winds until he was above the turbines.

While Carl and Hitomi crawled backwards through the grass, out of sight of the approaching cars, they could see the Don fly across a hill — and disappear behind it.

From a more remote position on top of a hill covered with low bushes, the bizz jockey and his producer looked down, but they could no longer see the entire area. The roaring of the engines was clear, but the cars were out of sight.

The wind seemed to be slowing down slightly for a while,

so they could have a normal conversation for a change.

"Lalo seems to be safe," said Carl. "But I think our first priority is to walk around this hill and get to him. He probably landed somewhere over there. Then we can come back and see what these people are doing."

"Could be maintenance," said Hitomi.

Carl liked to think that too.

Then, all of a sudden, the cars appeared again, blazing back the way they came.

In a hurry, Hitomi took out the binoculars from her backpack again. "Only drivers this time," she said to Carl.

"We better team up with Lalo," the bizz jockey responded, "And then find out what these men are up to, if they're not chasing us. Stay out of sight."

"If they were coming after us, they would have simply driven those land rovers up this hill," said Hitomi.

"They're probably here for a long picnic," growled her boss, "and I'm not the one who's going to serve them the mustard. Come on, we're outta here."

Then he held Hitomi's arm to stop her and said: "Can't we call him on his cell phone to try and find out where he is?"

"No. He doesn't have a cell phone."

Hitomi walked away quickly, bent over to stay low and out of sight.

"He's the godfather of paranoids," the bizz jockey mumbled.

Twenty-two

It took them a whole hour to regroup. Lalo Schilverstein had landed only a few hills away from their original point of view — but since they had no back-up plan, they did a lot of walking back and forth. Because none of them wanted to be spotted by the carloads of thugs in the area, they were keeping a low profile that proved impractical.

"If you hadn't been hiding in these bushes, we would have found you a lot sooner," Carl complained to Lalo when they finally got together.

"I wasn't hiding," said the Don. "I was busy liberating my glider from some thorny bushes without ripping anything."

"You're rich enough to not worry about ripping a kite," Carl said.

"I'm rich *because* I worry about ripping kites," Lalo snapped back.

"Any idea what these men are doing here?" said Hitomi. "Maintenance, perhaps?"

"Maintenance people don't drive so fast," said the Don. "They usually have all the time in the world. No, this is a whole different ball game. We're going to check it out."

"What?" said Carl. "Like, right now? Just like that?"

"We'll just peek over the top of the hill. From the bushes we can check out the area and see what they're doing."

"I think getting cozy with a couple of guys in black uniforms in the middle of nowhere, without the protection of a radio microphone or a TV camera, is a very bad idea," said Carl. "Come to think of it, it's the worst idea since the building of the Berlin Wall."

"Worse things have happened since then, my dear bizz jockey," said Lalo. "There are more walls today then there were during the Cold War."

"Be quiet," ordered Hitomi. "We are on our way right now. We can't rest until we know they're not after us. And if that is the case, we need to leave right away."

She started down the hill, but Lalo took a few steps back and took off his gear and put it down just below the hilltop. He shoved the backpack and the large pack that contained his hang glider firmly between the thick branches of a rhododendron.

Then he followed Hitomi, with Carl right behind him.

The field of towers was empty. There was no doubt about that. The tall machines soared above the ground, their rotating heads turned to the oceanic wind, oblivious to anything that happened at their feet.

Down there, tiny creatures crawled around from turbine to turbine.

"They stopped here," said Lalo, pointing to the tire marks in the dusty, sandy soil.

The imprints of the land rovers were clear: the cars had

arrived at some point and then all made wide-angled turns around several towers and had driven back the way they came.

"If they didn't leave in the cars and they didn't walk anywhere...," said Carl.

"Then they went inside one of these turbines," said Lalo.

"Maintenance?" said Pappas but he shook his head at the same time.

"It's this one," said Hitomi. She stepped on the concrete foot of one wind turbine.

"And why is that?" said Carl.

"Why, isn't that obvious?" laughed Lalo. He made a dancing movement, a clownish jumping under his flying white hairs.

"Enlighten me," said Pappas.

"This turbine is not only in the center of the circles the cars made when they turned. It is also in the exact center of the entire turbine field."

Lalo jumped onto the concrete floor of the turbine, which was half a meter high.

There was a metal door in the tower, with a lock next to it. Underneath the lock were a small screen and a keypad.

Schilverstein put his hand on the keypad and started typing like a maniac, producing rows and rows of digits on the small screen.

Whatever he was doing, the bizz jockey didn't get it. It made Hitomi smile her reserved smile and it resulted in the door popping open.

"I'm not sure that's a good idea," said Carl, deciding not to comment on yet another talent of Lalo Schilverstein as a regular Houdini. "There's a lot of people down there, if that's where they went."

"They're busy minding their own business," said Hitomi, while she followed the Don into the steel tower.

Once again, Pappas looked up to the giant blades looming over his head, which were whirling through the wind. The noise from on high almost equaled the din emanating from the machine's interior.

The bizz jockey sighed. What on earth had happened to his producer, who was usually quite prudent? Was she in love perhaps, and did the insane ideas of the Don Quixote madman infect her, and put her up to these crazy acts?

She's crazy to go in there, Carl thought, while he stepped into the darkness beyond the door. She's supposed to look after me, not the other way around.

But... what a story it might make!

He looked around him to check if anybody was watching them, and then closed the steel door behind them.

Twenty-three

Once on the inside of the steel tower, Carl had to wait a few moments to allow his eyes to adjust themselves to the darkness. There were small lights attached to places of special interest. In particular, a small box attached to the wall, like a metal medicine cabinet, with thick wires coming out the bottom, a ladder that went up into the tower, with a small service elevator platform about ten meters above them, and a stairway that went down.

Lucky for Carl, the stairway down was enveloped by a small wicket, which he stumbled upon. Once his eyes were comfortable again, he realized he was alone in there.

"Yo, Hitomi," he whispered. "Kite man?"

A hiss came from downstairs. "Down, bizz jockey."

While he carefully walked the spiraling stairs that clearly led underground, he answered: "What if they went up?"

But there was no answer. The bizz jockey heard vague noises coming from deeper down, the sounds of footsteps on the metal stairway. But there was also a loud humming of machines that turned the small, dark space into a claustrophobic place to be.

Also, the downward climb began to worry Carl after some time. There seemed no end to it. To say "no end in sight" would be incorrect, because the dim lights illuminated not much more than the spaces where you could set your foot down.

So that's all he could do for a long time; it felt like at least a half hour before Pappas reached the end of the stairs.

There, the Don stood on a steel floor in a tiny space that resembled the interior of an industrial elevator. As if he could read the bizz jockey's mind, he said: "We're at least a hundred meters under the surface now. Can you believe that?"

"Seeing is believing," said Carl dryly.

Then Hitomi opened the only door in the small space and peeked through. She turned and whispered: "I can't make anything of it, but at least I don't see any people."

The three of them left the cabin and walked into a wide space that was like nothing they had ever seen before in their lives.

Instinctively, Pappas thought of a way to describe the sight to his radio audience, if that moment ever came: think of an oil field, with all those giant pipes crossing the ground and going into the ground and coming out of the ground, large silos with grease dripping from the sides; and then a giant black roof placed on top of all that, with fluorescent tubes producing a pale, unnatural light, as if there's no sun.

"Whatever you do, don't smoke," said Lalo.

Which made no sense to neither Carl nor Hitomi, but what the heck.

The area was so large, they couldn't see where it ended.

Loud humming noises came from further down.

"It seems whatever kind of machines are at work, they're below us," said the Don. "So we'll have to carry on to shed some more light on this. One thing I can tell you though, this is not electricity they're generating here. This wind turbine is a complete fake; it stands waving its arms while hiding something completely different."

Carl waved an arm to dismiss that remark. "Yes and it's oil. I can smell it. Big deal. Why go further down, isn't it all totally obvious?"

"Not entirely," said Hitomi. "We still need to know where it's going." Having said that, she headed for another stairway and disappeared to the next level, followed by the Don.

"No, we don't need to know because it's easy to guess. Also it doesn't matter where it goes because it ends up in your car either way." Carl looked at the now empty entrance to the stairway down. "You guys do that. I'll stay here, sort of on the lookout."

A confirming grunt from Lalo Schilverstein came from below.

Another level down, the stench of oil and chemicals penetrated Hitomi and Lalo's skins and the sound of the machines droned through their bones.

They stood on a greasy metal floor, looking at huge pipes coming down, entering a wide silo, that was covered by a metal roof and mounted by pumps and other industrial equipment. Down here the light was the same, pale and rich with shadows.

"I think that's what we're looking for, over there," said Hitomi.

She pointed at a tunnel close by, big enough to allow the passage of three huge oil pipes and still leave ample room for people and vehicles to take the same route.

They walked towards the beginning of the tunnel.

"It's going down," said Hitomi.

"Yes. Just a bit though, just enough to head for the ocean floor," said Lalo.

"You think they...?" Hitomi started to ask, but she stopped halfway.

"We are thinking the same thing," said Lalo, but by then he saw a worried look on Hitomi's face and he realized why she had aborted her sentence.

He could hear people, shouting above the droning of the machines. There was also the roar of another engine approaching them.

In the tunnel, they saw shades. The long, vague shadows of men walking towards them. They moved like crooked giants along the tunnel's side.

Twenty-four

"Boys and girls of the international business community, I'll tell you a joke that's not for laughing at," Carl Pappas said.

He stood by the stairway, looking around him every now and then.

Because there was no one to be seen, he had resorted to creating some fine opening lines for his next business radio talk show episode. Even though he had his own staff writer, the talented Job Messner, he was adamant in contributing to the texts himself.

"There's an oil baron who wants to catch up with the times and do something good for the environment for a change," he said. "But he can't think of anything, because everything everybody else is doing is going to cost him money."

Pappas looked around for a moment. He heard noises, but he couldn't place them immediately.

Then he resumed: "So he lies awake at night, next to his new trophy wife, and he can't sleep and he goes down to his kitchen and opens the fridge to take out some ice cream — and then it hits him. He is going to store oil in orbit around the planet. Isn't that just brilliant? In a decade or so, when the world runs out of oil, he will have a huge stack of it floating in satellites around the planet. Out of the reach of governments and people. Then, when the oil is worth a fortune, he'll bring it down barrel by barrel. And the people are going to love him when it's literally raining oil! So he goes to bed again, all excited and he wakes up his new trophy wife and..."

The noise was getting louder, but before he could look down and see if it was indeed coming from where Hitomi and Lalo had gone, an alarm started to wale.

It was one ugly mother.

The bizz jockey's ears protested; there was no doubt that this type of alarm was meant for serious business. So he turned left, then hesitated and turned back to go the other way, backed off again, and finally stood still were he had been to begin with: next to the stairs.

Feverishly, Carl started to consider his options. They had to retreat out of this structure as quickly as they could, he thought, and hide in the countryside. The alternative would be hiding in here, in a dark corner, and waiting for the alarm to be shut off and the danger to subside. It all depended on whether they had been spotted — in short, he couldn't decide what would be the best thing to do, so he put his foot forward towards the stairs in a serious attempt to follow Hitomi and Lalo.

Precisely then, he saw them emerge from the lower level.

"Run for the exit," Hitomi hissed, pushing him back, taking his elbow and turning him.

"What happened down there?" asked Carl, as they rushed through the dark corridor.

"The whole team of ugly bouncers came in our direction," panted the Don. "They were in a tunnel that leads to the ocean. Unfortunately, we waited too long."

"Some were walking," added Hitomi. Her stride was the most powerful of the three of them. The two men had a hard time keeping up with her, though this was particularly true for the bizz jockey. Lalo Schilverstein was older, but he was no doubt in better shape. Flying around under a kite obviously does more for a man's vigor than sitting at a table, barking into a microphone. "So while we were making our minds up about a retreat, a car came from the same tunnel, a sort of buggy. It was too fast. We couldn't get away in time. So... they saw us."

They were now close to the door.

The Don stopped, with a wide grin on his face. "You guys start climbing. I have a very funny plan to win us some precious time."

When Carl and Hitomi were halfway up the stairway that took them to the surface, the lights went out.

"Great," said Carl. He stumbled immediately. "He calls that funny?"

"He must have caused a short circuit," said Hitomi. "No problem. Keep your hand on the railing and keep climbing step by step. It's a circular stairway, nothing can go wrong."

The bizz jockey followed her advice. "He could at least have given us a warning or something. Funny sense of humor."

"Yeah, he's great, isn't he?"

In the darkness, Carl put on a questioning mark on his face.

"It's a gas. Too bad you can't see my face in this pitch black."

"Hey, you're a radio man. I can do without the image."

In the darkness, they continued the climb. The sound of the alarm gradually faded as they progressed foot by foot.

But just as they reached the upper level and saw some light come through cracks in the metal construction of the turbine tower above them, they heard the door bang in the deep — and then the running of feet up the same metal steps.

Twenty-five

A storm was gathering.

Fortunately, it was giving Carl, Hitomi and Lalo some backup by pushing them away from the ocean as they ran into the surrounding hills.

But they knew this was merely a short delay of the inevitable. The thugs were going to catch up with them very soon, because there was no reason to believe those men would run any slower. The only one of them who could run fast and long, was Hitomi, and there was nothing she could do about the two men who tried to keep up with her.

After the first hill, it started to look bad.

Lalo had picked up his backpack and flying gear on the way and by then the bizz jockey complained about a pain in his spleen. He bent over and stood there for a moment.

The wind was less powerful here, but they saw black clouds among all the gray ones, and the high-pitch tones the air produced as it hovered through the bushes and along the rocks was a simple reminder of the toughest kind of weather coming their way.

Hitomi stood next to Carl and bent over as well, to check

his face.

Behind her, the Don said: "You guys disappear in the bushes and get away from this place. I'll organize a distraction for these men. You can trust me. Now go!"

It took a moment for these words to sink into Hitomi, who was concerned about her boss. By the time she realized what the Don had said and she looked up, he was already jumping up from the top of the hill.

"Lalo!" Hitomi shouted. "We don't need heroes!"

Without any delay Lalo's kite caught wind. For a moment it looked as if he wasn't going to fly but simply be blown away — but then he made a turn and slipped through the vents and currents up and around the hill.

Hitomi ran to the hilltop to look, but she saw the men running over the wind turbine platform in every direction, so she retreated immediately. She obviously had no choice.

"Where's Schilverstein?" creaked Pappas, when she teamed up with him.

"He's being a clown as usual," Hitomi said. "Never mind."

The athletic producer pulled the bizz jockey into the low foliage where they could proceed without being seen all the time. There were thorny shrubs here, but also harmless rhododendrons and birch trees. A strange environment, she thought, neither entirely subtropical nor entirely boreal. Something of both.

They felt safer among the bushes and trees, but that was not set to last. The wind finally unleashed its full strength.

===

The dust finally let go of the ground on Islasol. It had resisted the winds so far, being glued to the earth by recent rains, but all of a sudden it had lost what little cohesion it possessed and flew up into the air with unexpected enthusiasm. At the sight of this spectacle of whirling, jumping and exploding grains, Dervish dancers would go home and never dance again.

The entire show had been set up by the elements to come to the rescue of the modern day Don Quixote, Lalo Schilverstein, who was indeed in serious trouble.

He had been spotted by the men in black clothes, who swarmed the turbine platform looking for the intruders. One of them started screaming and they all turned, and looked at the giant wing hovering above them in its rocky flight. Lalo looked like he was going to crash any minute, but the men below him weren't planning on waiting for that.

Guns were drawn.

And while the first bullets whirled by him, the dust moved in with the wind, which turned and turned and circled the platform, and blurred all vision within moments.

The shooting ceased and the Don was carried above the cloud of dust. This time, his craftsmanship had nothing to do with it; he was ushered across the hills by the winds, which had taken over all control.

Lalo gasped for air — but he got nothing but a mouth full of dust. Sand had filled his eyes, for he had forgotten to use his goggles this time.

Branches of trees hit him in the face. His knees hit a rock and were fractured upon impact. A hollering voice from the wind accompanied his abduction.

Twenty-six

The *Parallel Line* was moving. The giant container ship was still almost empty, having only just been connected to the undersea oil pipeline a hundred meters below the surface. Its hollow hull echoed with the sounds of the storm and the rising waves.

Although the ship was too large to be in real danger at any time, the captain was standing on the bridge with a worried eye. In front of him stood a couple of monitors. Its black and white screens showed an underworld, a blurry dark deep sea with divers at work around a giant vertical pipeline, lit by giant strobe lights that brought even the tiniest plankton into view.

The captain rubbed his short beard and gulped some coffee as he stared. He was a tall man in a meticulous uniform, tidy and neat, as if he was about to perform a hero's part in a movie. He sat straight up in his captain's chair, but it was all outward calm. He did not like what he was seeing. Not one bit.

"There's too much movement," he said to Ben Bercovitch, who came barging on to the bridge, through one of the outer doors, inviting a part of the storm and the rain in with him.

"That's your problem," answered Bercovitch. "We have more serious issues ashore that we must deal with. Perhaps it's wise to call the whole thing off."

His eyes followed the captain's finger to one of the screens. "They're moving up and down with the current, big deal."

"The pipeline's connection to my ship is strong, but not unbreakable," said the captain. "You should be worried too. And what's going on ashore anyway?"

The boss slumped down in another chair and sighed. "People with clout nosing around. Perhaps it can be fixed. Perhaps some money will do the trick. Perhaps not."

"That's a lot of perhaps."

Bercovitch looked out the window, into the gray rain. "What's that?" he asked.

The captain looked up in horror. "It's a rogue wave!" He grabbed a microphone from a radio switchboard and yelled: "This is the captain. Shut down the pump and disconnect the pipeline immediately. I repeat: shut down the pump and dis..."

Then the giant wave plunged over the side of the ship. It washed the bridges window entirely, making the noise of a football stadium full of pissed off fans.

And even while the ship was built to withstand this kind of force, it did respond to it in some way, rocking in the ocean water, pulling its anchor and, with that, the oil hose that was connected to the pipeline on the ocean floor.

Red lights started to flash on the dashboard, close to the black and white underwater monitors.

Then the outside door opened again and members of the crew started to enter the bridge.

Twenty-seven

Lalo woke up in a total darkness. There was not a single part of his body that was not hurting, except for his eyes.

He felt the polyester canvas of his giant wing walk over his face and pushed it aside.

It was a bright night and a full moon stood among the stars. The storm had vanished in its entirety. There were no clouds but there was still a wind left, which blew across the island and brought fresh smells to his nose. The sweet aromas of frangipani and rhododendrons, and a whiff of salty air floated his way from the other side of the landmass.

The Don realized he had landed on the opposite side of Islasol. Across the water, in the distance, he could see the lights of the mainland.

The storm had blown him away from the band of thugs and the wind turbines and taken him many kilometers across land and plunged him on the edge of the island. But what had happened to his brother and sister in arms, the bizz jockey and his producer? He decided to waste no more time and to effect a rescue plan immediately.

If only he had a clue about a good back-up strategy, which

he hadn't.

The terrain was rough and uninhabited. Behind him were the rocky hills and in front of him was the beach. There were no people. The bright light from the moon made that clear enough.

But then he spotted a small fishing boat lying only a few meters from the beach, a couple of hundred meters from where he was sitting. In the ship's lights, Lalo saw a man wading through the water and walk onto the beach.

The man was coming towards him.

Getting up proved hard, one of his knees giving him an excruciatingly hard time, so the Don just waved at the man and waited for him.

"Dear me, what are you doing in this remote place, me boy," the man asked. He looked every bit the way a classic fisherman was supposed to look. Rough clothes, plastic boots covering his legs up and above his knees, whiskers and eyebrows the size of wildcats and a dead pipe in his mouth.

"It's a long story," said Lalo.

"I have time," said the fisherman. "I'm Rocco by the way."

"I'm Lalo. I'm very glad to meet you."

"I can see why. Are you hurt?"

"Fraid so," said the Don. "I may have broken something in my flight."

The man kneeled and touched the hang glider. "You flew this thing then, me boy? You must be the White Knight or something of sorts."

Then he got up. "Be best if I brought you somewhere then." But then he stood still and touched his chin and looked at the man with white hair. "Say, you wouldn't by any chance be that flying Don Quixote everybody is talking about, who painted deadheads on wind turbines on a nearby island recently?"

"I most certainly am," said Lalo.

"Don't worry, I'm with you all the way," said Rocco. "I think you are putting yer finger on a sore spot there, me boy. Now I'm going to help you get up and then we get to my boat."

While they started to get to work, Lalo said: "I don't mean to rush you, my dear man, but I am in a bit of a hurry. Some friends of mine were left behind in last night's storm and they might be in a tight spot."

"They won't be for long or my name is not Rocco Sirocco," said the fisherman.

The Don wanted to ask if his name was really Sirocco, because he thought it was sheer poetry to be named Rocco Sirocco, but the first excruciating pains of his next journey were announcing themselves. So he left it at that.

===

The bizz jockey awoke when the sun was appearing above the horizon. Although his head hurt like hell, he grabbed around him to get some support and hurt his hand in a thorny bush. While a soft cry escaped from his lips he got to his knees.

But before he could rise, he was grabbed by his belt and pulled down on the ground again with more force than he could withstand.

"What the..." he started, but a hand was put over his mouth.

"Be very quiet," said Hitomi. "We're not alone."

Then last night came back to Carl with full force. The run

from the wind turbine park, the maneuver by Lalo Schilverstein, the rising of the dust cloud and their escape into the hills. How they had stumbled on rocks and bumped into trees and thorny bushes, and then crawled on their knees to keep out of sight — and then nightfall.

"Where are they?" whispered Carl.

But Hitomi put an index finger to her lips.

Then a voice sounded, from an invisible mouth a few meters away: "Footsteps all over the place. They were here, no doubt about it."

Pappas felt his heart jump to conclusions.

"Don't shout, you moron," another voice hissed.

To Carl and Hitomi's horror, this second voice was even closer to them. With his lips, Pappas said "we have to go now", while he pointed away from the voices.

But then he saw Hitomi's face turn pale, and he looked in the direction he had just pointed towards — and looked right in the face of a tall man. No, he wasn't tall, he decided, this man was huge. The man was like a tree.

"Don't move a muscle," said the oak.

Twenty-eight

Through the bushes around them, more men appeared, all dressed in black, all wearing sunglasses, but none of them as huge as the oak.

But they looked mean enough, with their unsmiling faces, the corners of their mouths pointed downwards, their upper torsos ready to play walk-on parts in violent movies, and their automatic weapons pointed at the bizz jockey and his producer.

"My muscles have no serious plans for the foreseeable future," said Carl.

His remark drew no response whatsoever.

Hitomi rose in front of the oak. Even though the man towered above her by almost half a meter, she pinched him in the chest and said: "You better behave, bad boy. This man is the bizz jockey and there will be ten million angry listeners who will turn on you if anything happens to him."

There was a silence for a moment and then the men all laughed. By now there were at least eight. One started talking into a cell phone, there was the roaring of cars in the near distance and on top of it all, the oak struck Hitomi down. He simply slapped her in the face and she ate dust.

Pappas wanted to jump to his feet but Hitomi grabbed him by the arm and stopped him. He looked at her face, which turned red and pushed some blood out of the nose.

"Don't," she said.

Hands appeared from every direction and grabbed them and jerked them in an upright position. Next they were dragged rough handedly through the sand and the bushes.

"Get them in a car and out to the northern exit on the double," someone yelled. "And you guys, erase all these tracks. And you: check the entire distance between where we found them and the turbines for stuff they may have dropped. On the double, people. Within half an hour I want all traces of these two bozos gone from the face of the earth."

While they were dragged, their knees and feet bumping against rocks and tree trunks, Carl and Hitomi heard someone say something about "going off a cliff".

That's when the struggling began. Both Pappas and Sakamoto started kicking and screaming and moving their bodies up and down. The men who carried them, fell to the ground and they all started to wrestle.

"Separate them, we'll finish it here," the oak yelled.

Desperately, the bizz jockey and his producer fought and held on to the men.

"Let go!" someone yelled.

Then, a whole new set of sounds entered the arena.

A helicopter had apparently approached from behind the hills unseen and unheard, for it suddenly made a roaring noise right behind the closest slope, and then rose into the air. A little further, two more giant humming metallic insects appeared.

From a giant megaphone, attached to the belly of the first helicopter, a voice came like a thunderstorm.

"AAAND... WE'RE ON LIVE RADIO, HOVERING RIGHT OVER THE ISLAND OF ISLASOL. I WILL DESCRIBE THE SCENE FOR ALL OF YOU LISTENERS TO WCBN RADIO: THERE ARE AT LEAST A HUNDRED WIND TURBINES IN THE BACKDROP, RIGHT WHERE THE OCEAN STARTS. DOWN HERE ON THE GROUND, YOU ARE NOT GOING TO BELIEVE ME, STANDS THE WCBN RADIO BIZZ JOCKEY OF THE BOARDROOM, MR. CARL PAPPAS, WITH HIS PRODUCER RIGHT THERE WITH HIM, AND IT APPEARS THEY ARE SURROUNDED BY MEN IN BLACK. YES, THEY LOOK REALLY BAD TO ME, BUT WHO KNOWS IF THEY'RE THE BUSY BOYS OF SOME CRIMINAL CARTEL OR SIMPLY GOVERNMENT ENFORCERS? YOU CAN'T TELL THE DIFFERENCE ON FACE VALUE THESE DAYS, NOW CAN YOU?"

The men had stopped dragging Pappas and Sakamoto through the dust and the bushes and stood there looking up in utter confusion. The oak's mouth hung open and it turned out to be as big as every other part of his body — he looked as if he actually wanted to try and swallow one of the helicopters.

"What the..." someone muttered.

Simultaneously the bizz jockey and his producer were dropped to the ground. They thudded on the dusty soil and saw the men around them raising all kinds of weapons, from handguns to automatic rifles and Kalashnikovs and point at the helicopters.

From the megaphone a short WCBN Radio tune blazed in

their direction, and then the voice resumed: "AND WHAT'S ALL THAT THERE IN THE BACKDROP, WHAT'S THAT IN THE OCEAN? IS THAT INDEED A LARGE OIL STAIN ON THE BLUE WATERS OF ISLASOL? IS THERE SOME ILLEGAL OIL DRILLING GOING ON HERE IN ONE OF THE LARGEST NATURE RESERVES IN OUR PART OF THE WORLD? I'M TAKING MY BINOCULARS RIGHT NOW... AND... YES IT IS! I CAN SEE THE COLORS OF THE RAINBOW EMANATING FROM A HUGE BLACK CIRCLE ON THE OCEAN, AND TWO GIANT CONTAINER SHIPS MAKING THEIR WAY OUT."

The oak finally lowered his handgun and screamed orders at the men around him, who followed his example immediately. Guns were lowered. Then the whole band ran off, down the slopes of the bushy hill in the direction of the wind turbine park and their approaching land rovers.

"AND THE MEN WITH GUNS, THE MEN IN BLACK THAT WERE THREATENING OUR OWN WCBN RADIO'S BIZZ JOCKEY AND HIS PRODUCER, ARE NOW RUNNING OFF BECAUSE THEY HAVE BEEN EXPOSED. WELL, YOU KNOW WHAT THEY SAY: WHEN THERE'S OIL AND THERE'S MEN IN BLACK, SOMEONE'S GOT SOMETHING TO HIDE!"

"Is that Don in there?" Carl asked. His voice creaked like an old stairwell. "I think I see him!"

Behind the helicopter glasses, his personal sound engineer Don Wozniak could clearly be seen, his head stuck between the jaws of a giant headphone. In the front seat, next to the pilot, Lalo Schilverstein was holding a microphone in front of his mouth.

"No doubt about it."

"He has clearly lost his mind."

"He's simply executing another one of Lalo's great ideas," said Hitomi.

"How do you know?"

"Isn't that obvious? It's typical for his way of thinking. Don's got nothing to do with it, he just takes care of the technical side."

The helicopter began to descend, looking for an open space to land. The other machines started a pursuit of the fleeing band.

With the noise of the rotor blades subsiding and the dust clouds halting, Carl and Hitomi finally found the nerve to get to their feet. Hitomi jumped to it, re-energized by yet another inspired action from Lalo, while Carl hissed and puffed in the process of emerging.

The first thing they saw was the ocean in the distance, the two ships — that looked tiny from where they were standing — on the way out, and a dark spot on the water that looked like a mirror image of an eclipse of the sun: black and lifeless.

Twenty-nine

From his seat by the window of the plane, Ben Bercovitch saw the oil stain in the ocean. It shimmered in the morning sun reaching across two, maybe three kilometers in diameter, reflecting the sun's rays in a spectrum of colors.

All of the passengers appeared to be looking, except for the man sitting next to him. He was an unremarkable man, the kind you would expect to be working in the last room in an accountancy firm's hallway, checking the books five days a week, year after year, never complaining, never in a different mood than the other day. He wore short gray hair, a gray suit and gray glasses in a pale face.

But looks deceive, as always, for in the midst of the confusion the man whispered to Bercovitch:

"Better go and look out the window too, Mr. Bercovitch," he said. "You are attracting too much attention by acting so disinterested."

They looked each other in the eye.

Bercovitch sighed. He turned and looked out the window again, adding a few Ohs to all the Ahs that were sounding the cabins.

The gray man looked too.

"What's going to happen?" asked Bercovitch.

"They haven't decided yet," said the gray man. "You will probably get a new name plus a bank account somewhere in the southern hemisphere, or a one way ticket into oblivion."

"They're afraid I will talk? There's dozens of people involved, you can't hide them all."

"You are the only link between the governments and the oil, my man," said the gray man.

"Anything I can do to enhance my outlook on a healthy life?"

"No."

The plane was reaching its cruising altitude and the passengers were relaxing again, returning to their normal positions, some leaving their seats to walk through the aisle.

While unfolding a newspaper, the gray man chuckled. "Basically I am blocking your view," he said.

"Pardon?"

"Your outlook on a healthy life. I'm in the way. So if you wish to enhance your outlook, I'm the key."

So it's money he wants, Bercovitch thought.

He sat back, moved his chair into the lazy position and closed his eyes.

But it's true, he thought. I'm the one link nobody wants to see in court.

He fell asleep, trying to dream about a blue, shallow ocean by a blinding white beach, a lush tropical forest canopy climbing up a mountain and a white house between the palm trees, but by the time he was really dreaming, black crude oil gulfed on the beach, staining the white sand. A huge white seagull screamed at him, his feathers horribly glued together by the ancient gold of the earth.

Thirty

He didn't doubt it for a minute.

She's on the lookout for the Don Quixote, for Lalo Schilverstein, thought Carl. Right up to the moment when The Boardroom began, he saw her glancing at her cell phone, at the door, at the studio window, looking for the man with white hair to show up.

But he wasn't going to, obviously.

"You must improvise if he decides to show up," she had insisted an hour earlier.

"Hitomi, Lalo is not coming," Pappas had said. "He said he wouldn't. Remember?"

"He was just being polite," she had snubbed, "after you told him the show was a full house." But she hadn't looked convinced.

Apparently she was convinced now. As soon as the WCBN Radio announcer finished introducing the bizz jockey and The Boardroom started, she didn't look at her cell phone or the door or anywhere else, just at the studio table, where Carl was sitting with two young women and one man, engaging them in a lively conversation.

"You guys are the generation that will have to make all these environmental changes work, or it's the end of the line," he said. "My generation has done mostly talking, your generation will have to do most of the walking. You think it can be done?"

"It is being done right now, Carl," said one of the women, tall and robust and red haired. "Our startup is gaining momentum and it's all done through crowd funding. The people are deciding what to do about energy in the near future and by doing that they are reducing the stalwart influence of governments and the old-school energy companies like the oil giants."

"I'm not convinced," said Carl. "Doesn't the scheme we've just revealed in the Islasol nature reserve prove that the resistance to change is huge? That it's very difficult to overcome?"

"On the contrary," said the other woman at the table, who was bald headed, with piercings replacing her eyebrows. "You've actually heated things up for us. After all this publicity the public is a little bit more resolved than before to get this thing off the ground. And if you were worth your salary, you would dedicate ten minutes of your daily radio show for the rest of the year to support this."

Pappas eyed her solid appearance, a black sports suit enveloping her slightly overweight body, and the shining metal in her face, but he smiled while he was doing it — he liked the way she looked independent in a business world where most women tried to look like a president's wife, serious and decent. He believed that no one should be judged by their appearance, but if someone's looks could be judged in their favor, he jumped at the occasion.

"I'm a supporter, but The Boardroom is not participating in anything. We have to stay neutral. You guys will have to fight this. But I'll be talking about the wind turbine scheme many times in the coming months because the end is not yet in sight."

"The end?"

"Well, after the ocean has been cleaned up over there, which will take a few weeks, they'll be dismantling the oil drilling installation under the park and that will take months. We'll check the proceedings every now and then, send someone over to cover the latest developments. Also there's at least twelve governments looking into the people involved on two continents, so that's going to take some time. There will be an international trial, possibly even at the International Court of Justice in The Hague."

"Aren't you worried your audience may be bored after a while, Mr. Pappas?" the red-haired woman asked.

"I'm not worried because I *know* they'll be bored. That's how it goes," said Carl. "But I should be asking you: how will you keep public interest going, how are you going to keep the environment on the public agenda the way you've been doing?"

Awkward moments of silence never lasted very long in the presence of the bizz jockey.

"Oh let me guess, you guys are going to fix that with youthful enthusiasm," he said with plentiful of sarcasm in his voice, which further added to his guests' confusion.

Behind the main window, in the sound engineer's booth, Don Wozniak smiled.

But Hitomi Sakamoto, standing next to him, didn't smile. She looked at Wozniak and said: "Why are you laughing? Finally he's got some young, eager guests in his show, people that are going to make a difference in an indifferent world, and then he hits them over the head with sarcasm. Why is scaring away the good hearted so funny?"

Don looked up, surprised to hear such a long monologue from the producer, where he was used to her keeping things brief.

"Oh wait, I see," said Hitomi, "you're not really laughing. You're just having a cramp in your facial muscles after eating ten donuts in a row." She then walked out of the room towards the studio door, to be in time for the next break.

"Are you actually cóunting my donuts while I eat them?" he yelled after her.

He bent over the donut bag, looked at the remains, then at the receipt on his console.

Darned woman, he thought. That kind of accuracy is simply not normal. It should be looked into.

"And Carl wasn't being sarcastic," he mumbled.

Hitomi walked into the studio room without making a single noise. She entered from behind the three guests, so neither of them saw her come in. But the bizz jockey was acutely aware of her presence, and he noticed the look on her face in a way no one else could. For most people, the face of Hitomi Sakamoto betrayed nothing: it could be neutral at best and rigorous at most, but the impression was usually one of a mild disdain. That worked as a shield between the world and her boss, the bizz jockey; by keeping a straight face of disinterest, she could avoid a lot of small talk and all that other stuff that she and Carl referred to as radio ga ga. Guests were treated with a certain amount of neutral friendliness, colleagues received a more serious treatment, and if they were men they might even feel despised.

But Carl saw through all that and could actually read her face; at that very moment the Hitomi face told him to watch his big mouth.

So he switched to a different mode, motivated by the looks of Hitomi but also by the clock, that was counting down to The Boardroom's final moments of the day.

"I for one put great faith in you young people," he said. "There is no doubt in my mind that you are going to make a difference. And it is comforting to know that you will not be alone, because there's a guy out there who is looking after all of you, the guardian angel of everyone who wants to change the world for the better. So this is a call to all of you out there. Be on the lookout for the Don Quixote and his kite. Be on the lookout for Lalo Schilverstein anywhere where there's an environmental issue and if you see his graffiti, remember to keep your eyes open and think independently. Don't take that commercial crap about 'a better environment' at face value. There may be more to the picture than meets the eye."

All Carl got from Hitomi was a nod with the head. It was a giant acknowledgement that needed no emphasis. She was drifting off in her mind anyway, to the skies where a giant blue wing sailed on the wind, steered by a man with white hair sprouting from under his helmet. In her mind, his smile was just as white.

Power Play

***

Request from the author

Thank you for reading this Radio Detective adventure. I hope you enjoyed it and will be willing to write a review on the online platform of your choice. Making that extra effort is greatly appreciated by other readers... and of course by me. Thank you.

I hope you and I stay connected through Twitter, Facebook, Google+, Pinterest or my free email newsletter. I'll make sure you'll stay tuned.

Have a good evening/night/day!

M.H. Vesseur

Twitter @MHVesseur

Facebook www.facebook.com/MHVesseur

Subscribe to M.H. Vesseur's mailing list on
www.mhvesseur.com

About the author

M.H. Vesseur has written many short stories for literary magazines in The Netherlands, Belgium, Canada and the U.S.A. He was awarded for the best debut with his first story. In his radio detective series about Carl Pappas he has now written and published the seven short crime novels *CEO Groupie*, *Die Rich*, *Tax Me If You Can*, *Acid Asset*, *Nosedive*, *Power Play* and *Blood Border*. The radio detective's producer Hitomi Sakamoto now stars in her own series, which begins with *North*. M.H. Vesseur also published the novel *Lemniscate*, a collection of literary short stories called *Allusions* and his outlook on the super economy *Burning Neil Armstrong*. M.H. Vesseur is an awarded advertising copywriter. He lives in the forests of The Netherlands.

www.mhvesseur.com

Novels and ebooks by M.H. Vesseur

More information on:
www.mhvesseur.com/publications

Allusions (short story collection)
North (The Hitomi Files: 1)
Blood Border (a Radio Detective novel)
Power Play (a Radio Detective novel)
Nosedive (a Radio Detective novel)
Acid Asset (a Radio Detective novel)
Tax Me If You Can (a Radio Detective novel)
Die Rich (a Radio Detective novel)
CEO Groupie (a Radio Detective novel)
Beloved Stalker
Babyface Junkie
In Snuff Park
Sketches Of A Worldwide Christo And Jeanne-Claude
Narcissist Guru
Territory Game

Short stories by M.H. Vesseur

ALLUSIONS

Glimpses of tomorrow await you in this collection. The ultimate amusement park will offer you death. Everlasting youth will take you to the point of no return. The artificial landscape will fill you with joy if it doesn't scare the living daylights out of you. The Narcissist Guru will show you your many selves. There is the ultimate work of art that will change the planet and the old vaudeville star who is still being stalked. And finally, the coming of the super economy will haunt your dreams. This collection contains the short stories • In Snuff Park • Babyface Junkie • Narcissist Guru • Sketches of a Worldwide Christo and Jeanne-Claude • Territory Game • Beloved Stalker • Burning Neil Armstrong.

Available in The Hitomi Files by M.H. Vesseur

NORTH

Man should fear only one enemy

The only enemy who has the capacity to remove all of mankind from the earth, is the virus. Imagine the worst of them all, a true 21st century killer. It lies dormant in the remote laboratory of a pharmaceutical giant whose hopes of making billions off a vaccine somewhere in the future throw a dark shadow ahead. Then Hitomi Sakamoto, the hard boiled radio producer who's on a rough vacation in the wild nature of the north, stumbles upon this dark secret. She is drawn into a final battle between ruthless scientists, a greedy corporation, desperate but dangerous environmental activists, a cold-hearted assassin and... a manmade virus that longs to escape.

Hitomi Sakamoto first appeared in the Radio Detective novels by

M.H. Vesseur. Immediately popular for her iron work ethics and razorsharp tongue, Hitomi outgrew her boss (radio detective Carl Pappas) and now steps out of his shadow, into her very own adventure.

Available in the radio detective series by M.H. Vesseur

CEO GROUPIE - A radio detective novel

One night three live guests join Carl Pappas on his radio show The Boardroom: two CEOs and a woman who calls herself: "the CEO Groupie". When the mysterious woman reveals the existence of a secret call girl organization for CEOs and subsequently disappears a couple of days later, the bizz jockey engages on a search. What happened to the CEO Groupie and what are the other two guests up to? Together with his radio team — his producer Hitomi Sakamoto and his sound engineer Don Wozniak — Carl Pappas sets out to deal with this.

Available in the radio detective series by M.H. Vesseur

DIE RICH - A radio detective novel

Carl Pappas, the bizz jockey, goes on the air again. His radio show "The Boardroom" is both loved and feared by the global business community. He has a sharp eye for business news and the big mouth of a talk radio host. This time around he has some very wealthy guests joining him on his show: two billionaire entrepeneurs and their future successors, who also happen to be their sons. Of course it doesn't take the bizz jockey a very long time to upset some of his guests and his audience — and that same night the bizz jockey finds himself heading into dangerous waters, in the hands of some very angry rich people. His team — producer Hitomi Sakamoto and sound engineer Don Wozniak — is forced to go out and rescue their reckless boss. And then there are the rich kids they have to deal with...

Available in the radio detective series by M.H. Vesseur

TAX ME IF YOU CAN - A radio detective novel

Carl Pappas, the bizz jockey, is cooking up a real shocker: during a live broadcast of his popular business talk radio show "The Boardroom" he plans to reveal secrets about tax dodging practices around the globe. In the middle of the preparations he and his producer Hitomi Sakamoto face unexpected trouble. Who is trying to shut the Bizz Jockey up in this quiet country under the tropical sun? Is it the local military junta? Is it the business community? Or is the sun finally getting to Carl Pappas' head?

Available in the radio detective series by M.H. Vesseur

ACID ASSET - A radio detective novel

Carl Pappas, the bizz jockey, is feeling good about the prospects of environment-friendly plastics he's discussing on his radio show "The Boardroom". But as he soon finds out there's something not right with the company behind it. Can the bizz jockey protect a lonely scientist against the schemes of a large corporation that smells money? Or will he be unable to stop a revolutionary asset from becoming really acidic? Buckle up for a race against arsonists, corporate crime, dogs, bullets and a dangerous industrial zone in the middle of a blizzard, softened only by some real team spirit.

Also available in the radio detective series

NOSEDIVE - A radio detective novel

When a large corporation is struck by a cripling strike among its workers and an apparent terrorist attack on its factory, bizz jockey Carl Pappas steps forward to offer his public support. But as he soon finds out, there's more to the picture than meets the eye. Why is the owner hiding in her large mansion? What happened in her youth that is threatening her after all these years? It's a job for the radio detective — and this time around his boss gives an unexpected hand.

Available in the radio detective series by M.H. Vesseur

BLOOD BORDER - A radio detective novel

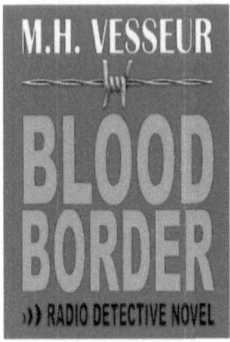

The inhumanity of human trafficking is forcing the radio detective to make a stand. So in the midst of politics and public outrage, Carl Pappas and his team infiltrate the trafficking cartel of a man known as The Clown. But there is nothing funny about it, for the radio detective soon finds himself in the lion's den, a place crowded with former narcotics traffickers and their violent ways. Will they be able to do something about the screaming injustice of immigration or will they become prey themselves?

<<<<>>>>